FINS

RANDY WAYNE WHITE

ROARING BROOK PRESS
New York

Copyright © 2020 by Randy Wayne White
Published by Roaring Brook Press
Roaring Brook Press is a division of Holtzbrinck Publishing Holdings
Limited Partnership
120 Broadway, New York, NY 10271
mackids.com

Library of Congress Control Number: 2019943528

ISBN: 978-1-250-24465-9

Our books may be purchased in bulk for promotional, educational, or business use. Please contact your local bookseller or the Macmillan Corporate
and Premium Sales Department at (800) 221-7945 ext. 5442 or by email at
MacmillanSpecialMarkets@macmillan.com.

First edition, 2020
Book design by Cassie Gonzales
Printed in the United States of America by LSC Communications,
Harrisonburg, Virginia

10 9 8 7 6 5 4 3 2 1

For my three favorite shark taggers, all saltwater borne:
Silas William Wayne, Saylor Grace, and
Emerson Elora White

ONE
LIGHTNING STRIKES!

After a few weeks in Florida, Luke decided he wanted to be a fishing guide like his aunt, Captain Hannah Smith, and was learning faster than usual until the day he was struck by lightning.

That's what he was told, anyway, by the old man standing over him when he woke up. By then it was raining hard.

"You okay?" the old man asked.

Luke blinked water from his eyes and croaked, "Huh?"

When the man's mouth moved to repeat the question, his words were muffled by a terrible ringing sound. "Huh?" Luke said again.

"My lord, you're deaf as a rock, but at least you ain't

dead." The old man exhaled and extended his hand. "Come on—get up."

Luke realized he was curled on a wooden dock, where he'd been watching a storm sail across the bay. The colors of the sky—neon green and purple—were unlike anything he'd seen while growing up on a farm in Ohio. Something else he'd never seen was a large, dark shape beneath the water—and what might have been the tip of a fin. An animal of some type cruising through the shallows toward him.

"What happened?" he asked when he was on his feet.

The old man pointed and spoke louder—or maybe the ringing noise was going away. "A lightning bolt hit close to where you were standing. Seemed to snake up out of the water and zapped you, too. I saw it all from the porch and come on the run. You okay?"

The man was short and wore thick glasses. Water poured off his straw hat like a waterfall. Luke couldn't understand why everything was blurry and why splotches of bright colors—neon green and purple—flickered behind his eyes.

"I feel sorta weird," he said, shaking the numbness from his hands. "Who are you?"

The old man appeared concerned. "You don't know?"

Luke squinted and tried to remember, despite the

swirling colors. "A fisherman, I think," he said finally. "Captain . . . Arlis something. Arlis Futch?"

The man took him by the arm. "You weren't the sharpest hook in the box to begin with, but now I'm worried. Come on, let's get out of this rain."

Luke was on the porch, a blanket around him, staring at an oddly shaped blister on his hand when Captain Futch came out of the house carrying a steaming mug.

"I'm too young to drink coffee," Luke told him.

"I'm not," the man said, "and I'm too old to be running around in a dang storm that coulda got us both killed. You just sit there and take it easy. Down the road we'll discuss an old saying about fools and ducks coming in out of the rain. Is your memory coming back?"

"I don't remember losing it," Luke replied.

"If you were the clever type," the man said, "I'd think you're being a smart aleck. How do you feel?"

"Like I stepped on a nest of hornets," the boy said. "I couldn't breathe—and my body was on fire. But I'm okay now." After a moment he added, "I saw something out there. From the dock. Big. Too big to be a fish."

"Son, in Florida there ain't nothing too big to be a fish. And making up stories is a piddly poor excuse for standing out in a storm." The man glanced at his watch as if awaiting the sound of a siren.

Luke didn't like that. "You shouldn't have called her," he argued.

The man was confused. "Who, your aunt Hannah? She don't answer the phone when she's on a fishing charter. You should know that by now. That woman's all business in a boat. When this squall starts to slide south, I'll try then."

"Not Hannah—the doctor who told you to call an ambulance," Luke said. He scratched at a painful area on his arm and kept talking, despite the look of surprise on the old captain's face. "Dr. Tamiko had to say that because most doctors are worried about getting sued."

The man squinted through his glasses. "How'd you know? You never met Doc Tamiko. Doubt if I ever mentioned her name before."

"You must've had the phone on speaker," Luke reasoned. "I heard every word she said. She told you to make us some hot tea while we waited. But she didn't mention making coffee for yourself and pouring whiskey in it. Oh—and that I should be checked for burns."

Captain Futch looked at the door to the house. It was closed. Through a window, he could see a fireplace and then a hall, which led to the kitchen, where he'd spoken in whispers to the only doctor on the island.

"If that don't beat all," the old man said. "Ten minutes ago you were deaf as a tree stump, and now you can hear through walls. Tell the truth—did you sneak inside when I wasn't looking?"

Luke wasn't sure how he'd heard the conversation from the porch during a rainstorm, but he had. "I don't need an ambulance," he said, getting up. "I feel okay now that my feet stopped stinging. Sorry you had to go out in this storm because of me, mister."

The old fisherman watched the boy start toward the door. "Where you think you're going?"

"Home," Luke said, "to put on some dry clothes."

"Home *where*?" the man asked carefully.

"You've never heard of the place—it's a little farm town west of Toledo. In Ohio. I don't mind walking in the rain."

"How do you feel about walking through snow?" the man inquired. This stopped the boy in the doorway. "Son, Ohio's a thousand miles north. If it's true that lightning never strikes the same person twice, I reckon you'll be safe as far as Kentucky—but I'd pack a pair of mittens. I need to tell you something before you hike back to the Buckeye State."

As Luke started to respond, he heard a buzzing sound, followed by an explosion of sparks in an oak tree visible from the porch. Thunder shook the house. He didn't flinch—seemed unafraid in a squall fired by lightning bolts and rain.

Captain Futch noticed and thought, *That boy was scared of his own shadow yesterday!* Then he said for Luke to hear, "I can give you two reasons you should stay and wait for the doctor. Take a look around. Do you remember being on this porch before?"

The pulsing colors in Luke's head dimmed while he squinted and tried to think. Inside the house a baby began to cry, frightened by the thunder. "Who's that?" he asked.

"That's your cousin, baby Izaak," the old man said, "so have a seat and don't argue. Luke . . . I'm your grandpa. You've been living here for close to a month."

Before he was struck by lightning, Lucas O. Jones was average, or below average, at most things, except baseball and farmwork. He wasn't bright, and he knew it. In Ohio, his mother and teachers had let him know often enough, but in a kindly way that took the form of excuses.

"He's easily bored," they would say, as if Luke wasn't in the room. "All children react to challenges differently." Or "His mind is so active, it tends to wander."

That was true. Sort of. He was prone to wander off in a dreamy way that seldom invited his brain to tag along. Once, he'd set off following fresh deer tracks in the snow. He didn't realize he had crossed the border into Michigan until a smiling state trooper informed him he was fifteen miles from home.

He often forgot important items: his lunch, his homework, even his catcher's mitt. It was a fine Wilson A2400, the professional model, that he'd baled hay most of a summer to buy.

"The little doofus would forget his head if it wasn't attached," his stepsister, who was not kind, had said more than once.

His stepfather, who was worse, had warned him, "If you don't smarten up, I might forget my promise to your mom and send you to live with your crazy old grandpa and that aunt of yours. She's not the sort to tolerate your bone-headed ways. Trust me, you wouldn't like Florida—nothing but heat and bugs and snakes down there. The place where they live isn't anything like Disney World."

That was a bad thing? Luke had been a kid, maybe seven years old, when his mother had taken him to Orlando. He'd hated the crowds and noise. Disney World sucked compared to this island on the Gulf of Mexico, where he'd been struck by lightning and was learning to fish but had yet to see a snake.

That was a disappointment. Luke didn't know much about reptiles but liked animals. They were a lot easier to get along with than people. He'd raised pigs, Black Angus steers, and a brood of chickens, and trained several dogs as 4-H projects. He figured a snake might be an interesting creature to have around.

Which is what he should've told his stepfather the day Luke forgot to shut off a tractor that, somehow, popped into gear and rolled into the pond. There'd been a bunch of yelling, then another threat when his stepfather hollered, "If I could afford it, I'd fly you south to live with your *real* family for a year. I swear I would."

Grandpa Arlis Futch was right—Luke wasn't clever enough to sass an adult. But he was a hard worker and good at saving money.

Luke had looked up at the man who wasn't his real father and said politely, "How much does an airplane ticket to Florida cost? I'll pay my own way."

That was in April. A snowstorm delayed his flight from Cleveland, and landing in the heat and sunlight of Florida had been like parachuting from winter into July.

A few weeks later—*zap*. Lightning struck. Now the boy's memory, like a computer, was beginning to reboot. Flickering strands of information took form in his head. Familiar images reappeared, then whole files—yet with blanks here and there.

"You'll be fine, Luke," Dr. Tamiko reassured him on a Friday. They were in her office. Through the windows he could see palm trees, where parrots and crows rioted in the shade. He had removed his shirt so the physician could inspect the odd burn marks on his shoulder and the palm of his right hand. She was a nice lady, not much taller than Luke, who was average in size for a sixth grader. But he was stronger than most because farmwork required lots of heavy lifting.

Now he was buttoning his shirt while she talked.

"The burn marks were caused by the lightning," she said. "Electricity. High voltage. It probably entered through your hand and exited from your shoulder. The blisters seem to have healed nicely." She noticed the boy's look of embarrassment and tried to reassure him. "Don't worry, the marks will fade as you age. And they're actually quite beautiful. Don't think of them as scars. They're more like pieces of art created by nature. Have you studied them closely in a mirror?"

Yes, Luke had. That's why he had chosen a long-sleeve shirt on this warm spring day. And why he kept his right hand closed to hide the strange, feathery-looking scar on his palm.

Dr. Tamiko said, "It was what the lightning did to your brain that worried us. You see, the human brain is what we call a chemo-electric organ. Studies have been done on people who've survived lightning strikes. It sometimes causes, well, changes in how they think and feel—even certain abilities. But you should be back to normal in a week or two."

"Chemo-what?" he asked.

"An electrical circuit," the doctor explained. "You said you were good at fixing engines?"

He wasn't good at it, Luke said, but he'd kept a lawn mower running, plus a chainsaw and the family tractor. He'd had no choice if he didn't want to do all the work by hand.

"The tractor was diesel," he clarified. "That's why I didn't think it was a big deal when it rolled into the pond. Diesels don't have carburetors."

"A pond?" the woman asked. "This is the first time you've mentioned what life was like before moving to Florida. Good, you're becoming more talkative, willing to engage." She made a note on a pad before looking up. "Talking openly about your . . . how your life was on the farm is a positive change from what I was told. The engine didn't get wet, I hope."

"Just on the outside," Luke said. "That was after I jumped in the seat and down-shifted. Then the whole tractor flipped and sank to the bottom. It's a pretty deep pond—even for a John Deere."

"You're saying you sunk a tractor?"

Luke nodded. "Not on purpose. I should've held my breath and tried to drive it out."

"Drive a tractor underwater across the pond?" Dr. Tamiko was skeptical.

"In low gear," the boy agreed. "I told my stepdad the same thing, but he was too mad to listen. The engine was still running because, like I said, it was a diesel."

Adults had a way of rolling their eyes that confirmed he wasn't bright. The doctor, unaware that Luke was right about diesel engines when submerged in water, smiled at him in a tolerant way.

"Back to what we were discussing," she said. "Thank goodness that bolt of lightning wasn't a direct hit. It would've killed you. Keep that in mind. Lightning kills more people in Florida than any state in the nation. But it hit close enough to short-circuit your brain . . . temporarily. Sort of like crossed wires in one of those engines you fixed."

She motioned to a screen where there were images of Luke's skull made by a device that had *bing*ed and clunked and rattled as he lay alone in a narrow tube. "The specialist we sent you to says that, in some ways, you might be more sensitive for a while to sounds, certain odors and colors— especially colors. Is that true?"

The boy sat straighter. He was interested but didn't want to show it. "Maybe," he said.

"Maybe?"

Luke nodded.

"Are you saying you *have* noticed a change regarding your sense of smell or how you see colors? The woman waited through a long silence. "Luke, it's not a bad thing. In fact . . . well, you might be one of the very few lightning-strike survivors who . . . Well, let me ask you some questions. First, what about your sense of smell. More sensitive?"

The boy's nose tested the room. Couldn't help it. The odor of a hospital was familiar—latex gloves, alcohol. The shampoo Dr. Tamiko had used that morning also hung in the air. There was a sharper scent, sort of like a locker room. Luke looked at his shoes and realized he should've changed his socks before leaving the house.

"My nose seems to work okay," he said, sliding his feet under his chair.

The doctor was encouraged. "Okay, what about colors? For instance, do words come into your head as if you are hearing them in color? I know that seems strange, words having color—unless I'm right. The same can be true of sounds and numbers. You might find you see all sorts of things differently now."

The boy shrugged. "Could be. Sort of, I guess."

Dr. Tamiko nodded as if pleased. "Really?"

"Yep. Colors. Sometimes."

"Excellent," the woman said. She made more notes on a pad.

Luke feared he'd said too much. "I guess that means I'm even weirder than I was to begin with."

"Weird? Why would you say such a thing?"

He didn't want to go into how many times his stepsister had called him that. "Are you going to tell my granddad and Captain Hannah?"

"Your aunt? Not if you don't want me to. But, Luke, listen to me." The woman placed her notepad on the desk. "There's nothing weird about the way a person thinks or feels—especially someone your age. Associating colors with words is nothing to be afraid of. Quite the opposite. A tiny percentage of people are born with a . . . well, let's call it a gift. A heightened sensitivity to almost everything. That's the way some describe it."

As she continued, a hint of excitement came into her voice. "Research suggests these people can sometimes see and understand what very few other people can, thanks to a . . . well, almost a sixth sense. Do you know what our five normal senses are?"

Maybe. Luke was reluctant to guess. He'd missed the

last two weeks of school, so it had been a while since he had failed a test.

The doctor let it slide. The five senses many humans possess, she said, are the ability to see, hear, touch, smell, and taste.

"This sixth sense that a few people seem to have," she added, "is very rare. It's usually associated with colors, certain sounds that only they can see or hear. There's a term for the condition. It's called synesthesia. Would you like me to write it on a piece of paper?"

"Sin-us-what?" Luke asked.

"Syn-es-thes-ia," the doctor said, pronouncing the word slowly. "Luke, listen carefully. Diagnostic tests show there have been changes in the frontal lobe of your brain that . . . well, it's complicated. But nothing to be afraid of. You're fine. The consensus is that the condition might be only temporary. With treatment, you'll soon be back to normal."

"Treatment?" Luke didn't like the sound of that. "What kind of treatment?"

"Don't worry about it now. What I'm telling you is, a team of specialists has reviewed your case. They agree you're going to be okay. Isn't that great news?"

After two weeks of dealing with doctors, Luke feared that if he spoke honestly, it would mean more brain scans, more testing—and maybe *treatments*.

"Sure, great," he said, which wasn't a lie exactly, but close.

The truth was, he didn't want to return to normal.

On the desk facing Dr. Tamiko was a laptop computer. Luke stared at it for a moment. A bluish color floated into his head. In the first few days after being struck by lightning, the appearance of this smoky-blue circle behind his eyes had scared him. But now he had come to think of it as a sort of "lightning eye" that he could focus almost like a telescope. "Uh . . . do you want me to answer those questions now?" he asked, referring to the computer screen. "Or do I have to come back?"

The look of suspicion on the woman's face told him he'd done something wrong.

"Were you snooping on my computer before I came in? Or . . . no," she decided, "you couldn't have. You don't know the password." This time her smile was sly and inquisitive. "I bet you cracked the door and listened while I was on the phone with the specialist. Am I right?"

"Sorry," the boy said. "It's rude to snoop."

"Eavesdropping," she said, smiling. "I thought so."

Luke didn't have to eavesdrop to know about the list of questions. On the wall was a mirror. It showed a reflection of the doctor's laptop screen. The list would have been a blur to most, and the sentences were reversed. But his lightning eye had unscrambled it all at a glance.

"Sorry," he said again, but didn't mean it. He was growing accustomed to a surprising change in his ability to hear and see, and to recall details of what he chose to remember. Sometimes, not always, his lightning eye could snap a photo that was filed away in his memory. The change had something to do with colors that still flashed in his head.

Luke didn't understand how it had happened, but for the first time in his life, he wasn't average. And he was no longer afraid of . . . well, just about everything in the world that was new or different. He didn't want a bunch of doctors messing it up.

"I'm in sort of a hurry," he added. "I guess I was trying to move things along."

"I don't blame you," the woman said. "Someone your age, cooped up in a doctor's office on a day as nice as this. You want to get outside and enjoy the first week of summer vacation, I suppose."

"No, ma'am," he said. "I've got a job interview this afternoon."

"Oh?" Dr. Tamiko put on reading glasses and focused on the laptop. "Captain Futch—your grandfather—he told me that's one of your other . . . uh, unusual qualities. That you're very independent for someone your age. Even before the lightning storm. What sort of job are you applying for?"

"Independent?" Luke asked.

"You'd rather work than play, in other words," the woman said, still focused on the computer. "He also said that you're shy and prefer to work alone. Is that true? You don't seem shy to me. There's nothing wrong with a child your age having fun."

In the hospital, a few days before she died, Luke's mother had told him, "Work hard, pay your own way, and you'll never owe anyone anything but kindness. Even your stepfather. Understand?"

Not at the time. But Luke was starting to get it.

He said to the doctor, "There's nothing fun about an adult deciding what I need—or if I deserve something I want to buy." He said this politely, then forced himself to make eye contact, something a shy, troubled boy would not do.

The woman was serious for a moment, saying, "A very good point," then laughed and asked again, "What kind of job are you after?"

"Tagging sharks and some other stuff," Luke replied. "There's a marine biologist who lives on Sanibel Island. My aunt Hannah, she's a famous fishing guide, and they're friends. I talked to him this morning, and we're going out in his boat this afternoon. Do you want me to answer those questions now?" He was referring to the list of questions on the laptop.

Dr. Tamiko was pleased by what she'd heard. She pushed the computer away. "I think you just did answer them, Luke," the woman said. "I'll have the front desk make a follow-up appointment. Let's say in a month?"

TWO
SABINA AND MARIBEL

When Sabina, who was ten, told the marine biologist, "I have no friends, no money—and the kids at school think I'm a witch," the man only smiled and asked, "Are you?"

"Am I what?"

"A witch?"

"A *brujita*?" The girl glowered and touched a string of beads. They were tiny blue and yellow cowrie shells that she always wore around her neck. "People think witches are old and ugly," she said. "Are you saying I'm ugly?"

The man laughed. "Your English is improving. But your attitude needs work."

It had been only a year since Sabina Estéban and her sister, Maribel, had left Cuba on a raft. It had been only ten months since an official in Miami had signed papers that made it legal for Mrs. Estéban to stay and work in Florida and for the girls to attend school. Sabina hadn't had much time to learn a new language—plus, she hated studying. That's why she'd misunderstood the biologist when he said something "needs work."

"I don't like to work," she replied in Spanish. "I'd rather read or write in my diary. If you're offering me a job, I guess I don't have a choice—but you'll have to pay me. What kind of job?"

Amused, the man removed his glasses and cleaned them with a towel. Nearby, several aquariums bubbled with color and life. There was a microscope on the table. On the wall, bottles of chemicals and test tubes were neatly lined in racks. The man was a biologist who studied fish and crabs and sea creatures of all types. He had helped Sabina's family become legal residents in this new country, where everyone, it seemed, was rich.

"You're the third kid today to ask about that job," he said in English. "I have something in mind, but it would require training—and a positive attitude. Are you willing to learn if your mom says it's okay?"

"I'm not a kid," the girl said, "and my attitude is none

of your business." A moment later she added, "Unless I didn't understand the words you used—it's possible. What does *attitude* mean in Spanish?"

"It means stop complaining and get busy."

"Busy doing what?"

"That's for you to decide," he replied. "Follow me."

The man, Dr. Marion Ford, lived in an old house built over the water, with a view of the bay on all sides. They exited the room and went down the steps to a platform that was also a dock, where a boat was tied. A wooden walkway angled toward shore. A large, curly-haired dog named Pete slept in the shade there. In deeper water, nets created a sort of corral.

"Are you interested in tagging sharks?" The biologist, peering down into the water, waved the girl closer to see. "There's a new research program for kids your age. I've been asked to participate. While you're learning, I could use some help around the lab."

It was a bright spring morning on Sanibel Island, on the west coast of Florida. Along the shore were coconut palms and tall white birds wading in the water. At the dock's edge, Sabina stared downward and saw three dark shapes cruising beneath the surface—fish of some type. They resembled miniature rockets with wings. The fish had dark, sleek dorsal fins and long sweeping tails.

"*Tiburones*," she said in Spanish, taking a step back. Much, much larger fish called *tiburones* had circled their raft on the voyage from Cuba.

"Sharks," Dr. Ford translated. "I caught them last night so I could demonstrate what you're getting into. You're not afraid to learn, are you?"

Sabina had a temper. That was why she was often in trouble with her mother and teachers, or Maribel, her superior-acting older sister. "I'm not a fool, either," the girl said. "Play tag with sharks? Tag's a game for children, not fish with teeth. I get teased enough at school without you teasing me about a job."

The biologist was a large, kind man with sharp eyes. Sometimes those eyes hid what he was thinking—even from Sabina, who had a gift for knowing what was in the minds of adults. It was not the only reason kids at school thought she was a witch.

Patiently, the man explained, "Tagging sharks isn't a game. You and your sister have more experience on the water than most adults. I've seen you handle rental boats around the marina. I think you're qualified for the tagging program I mentioned."

"*Maribel?*" The girl frowned. "I should've known. Did she already take the job? She has to be first at everything."

"Maribel was the second person to apply," the man said. "The first was a boy, probably a year or two older than you. I'm not sure. He grew up on a farm somewhere in the Midwest. Doesn't know squat about boats and fishing, but he knows a little bit about engines. And he's a strong swimmer. I tested him today at the beach. Maybe you three can work together."

"Doesn't know squat? That can't be good," Sabina said. She sensed the word's meaning but needed time to think. She didn't want to work with her superior-acting sister and a boy she'd never met.

"Florida's new to him," Dr. Ford said. "His grandfather's a friend of mine. Same with his aunt, Captain Hannah Smith. You've met her. She's one of the best fishing guides in Florida." He pointed across miles of blue water to an island. "They live over there. You might have fun showing a new kid the area."

"I doubt it," the girl said. "He must be rich to have a grandfather who lives on an island. Why does he need a job?"

"You live on an island," the biologist reminded her. "It's not always about money. His name's Lucas Jones—Luke. A few weeks ago, he got caught in a thunderstorm and . . . anyway, I have my reasons. The job's not just tagging sharks, understand. Taking care of my dog and feeding the fish when I'm away, that's most of it. Whatever work needs to be done around here, I'd rely on you."

"On *me*."

"That's right," Dr. Ford said.

Secretly, Sabina liked the biologist. He was quiet and was absentminded in a way that made her worry he might fall off a dock or forget to eat if someone wasn't around to take care of him.

"In that case, I accept," she said. "But don't blame me for my bossy sister's mistakes. Or for a farm boy who doesn't know squat. Does he speak Spanish?"

"He's willing to learn. That's part of the deal I made with him. He starts learning Spanish while you and your sister work on your English."

"Maribel's English is perfect," the girl replied. "That's

what the teachers say. Everything about Maribel is perfect. Just ask her."

The man gave the girl an affectionate look. "You've got to promise me something. If I hire you, no name-calling or squabbling with your sister. Not here, and especially not on the boat. I'll warn you once, and only once. Understood?"

Sabina felt her face warming. Maribel, with her long legs, her long black hair, and her quiet smile, was everyone's favorite. Even the biologist, as wise as he was, didn't understand how difficult it was to live with a sister who was pretty and smart and who never got into trouble.

Sabina was tempted to fire back, *No wonder you live alone with a dog, and no one to take care of you!*

Instead she nodded meekly. "I understand."

"Good." Dr. Ford grinned at her for a second, his mind already on something else. "Come back here in an hour, dressed for fishing—but only if your mother says it's okay."

Maribel Estéban was thirteen but felt older because of the responsibility that came with being the eldest in a single-parent family. Her mother worked second shift at a restaurant a few miles down the road. Her sister, Sabina, when she wasn't lazing around with a book or writing poetry, stayed busy irritating adults—which, Maribel knew, could lead to the worst kind of trouble.

The worst had almost happened back in Cuba. That was why her family had had to leave Cuba in a rush, then spend weeks in Miami so they could live legally in the States. It had been a long, confusing process with a happy ending—so far.

For Maribel, Florida was home now. She had worked hard at learning English and getting good grades because she feared disappointing her mother even more than failing in class. That was not the only reason. All her life, she had lived with a voice in her head that nagged and criticized and whispered that whatever she did wasn't quite good enough. The voice was always there. It was a shadow that taunted the girl even at the happiest of times. It constantly reminded her that she wasn't as smart or as confident as she pretended to be.

This had not changed since Maribel's earliest memories.

And her sister was a constant worry. Sabina had a temper and wasn't afraid to speak her mind. Worse, the girl had a spooky gift for knowing exactly what her enemies were thinking. And her enemies included just about anyone who didn't agree with Sabina's point of view.

The one exception was Dr. Ford. Like everyone at the marina, her younger sister was fond of the biologist. At times she would listen to him when she listened to no one else. This was evident from her cheery mood on their boat ride across the bay that afternoon. Maribel knew that the biologist had warned Sabina to be on her best behavior by the sly way her sister greeted the new boy, Luke, who was waiting for them on a rickety old dock a few miles away.

"How nice to meet you," Sabina said, as if practicing a phrase from an English book. "I think it is a beautiful day. Do you think it's a beautiful day?"

Luke stepped down into the boat. He nodded to both girls without making eye contact and spoke to the biologist. "I brought water and gloves like you said. Need anything else from the toolshed? I can run and get it."

He was already wearing gloves when he motioned to an old house built on a hill among trees on the bay.

The new boy seemed eager to please, as obedient as Dr. Ford's dog, a retriever they'd left back on Sanibel. And

Luke was quiet, not at all like the loud, clumsy boys at school. Maribel was relieved.

"Take a seat and hang on," the biologist instructed the boy. He indicated a spot next to Sabina, then changed his mind. "Keep Maribel company, and stay seated until I say you can move. When we stop, I'll go over the safety rules. Then we'll try to catch some sharks. Any questions?"

"Not from me," Sabina replied in a way meant to irritate.

Maribel glanced at Luke. She wondered if she should warn him that her sister, although often sweet and caring, had a sharp tongue.

When the boat was moving fast, the boy spoke, his voice just loud enough to hear over the noise of the engine. "Don't worry," he said. "I will."

"Will what?" Maribel asked.

"Ignore her," Luke said.

That's exactly what Maribel was about to say: *Ignore Sabina.* How had he known?

Before she could ask, the boy turned to watch seagulls trailing the boat across the water. "I ignore everyone when I'm learning something new. For some kids, learning new stuff is easy. Not me. My grandpa says I'm not the sharpest hook in the box."

Maribel didn't understand a lot of American slang. She took it to mean the boy was slow to learn—not a mind reader. That, too, was a relief.

Her eyes moved from Luke to her sister. Sabina was never without her necklace of blue and yellow beads. She'd bought it in a strange little shop outside Havana. There, the *santeras*—the women dressed in white, as they were sometimes called—had treated Sabina with rare affection and respect. The *santeras* were revered by many in Cuba. They practiced the healing arts, which, it was whispered, included magic.

One witch in the boat, Maribel decided, was trouble enough.

THREE
SHARK-FIN SOUP

The Estéban sisters, Luke realized, knew a lot about boats. He could tell by the comfortable way they moved, opening a hatch and coiling rope when the biologist told them, "Get the anchor ready."

"Want me to do anything?" he asked the man.

A simple shake of the head was the reply.

It was hot, but the sun felt good on this, the second day of summer vacation. What made it feel even better was that it was sleeting and cold back in Ohio, according to weather reports. Luke had checked that afternoon while waiting for Dr. Ford and the sisters to arrive.

Now here he was, in Florida, a strange land, in a boat

with a couple of girls who knew a lot more than he did, which was okay. He was determined to learn.

When the engine was off, anchor line taut, the biologist placed a block of frozen fish called chum in a bag. He tied it to a cleat and hung it over the side. The bag sank in a cloud of scales and fishy oil that created a slick on the water. Slowly the oil slick broadened behind the boat. The slick drifted with the tide toward deep water at the mouth of the bay.

Fish of all types, the man explained, are equipped with sensory organs that can detect the odor of food from far away. And none are better equipped than sharks.

"I want you to understand why tagging young sharks is important research—not just in Florida, but around the world," the biologist said. He waited to make sure he had the attention of Luke and Sabina before adding, "You kids can help with that research. You really can. Look around: What do you see? Water, right? Same with most people. But this bay is a lot more than water. This is one of the state's most important nursery grounds for all sorts of fish—especially young blacktip sharks. If we catch one, you'll see why they're called blacktips."

Every winter, he continued, schools of blacktip sharks

migrate south from the Carolinas to warmer water along the Florida coast. For them, shallow bays became nurseries. In summer, many blacktips return north.

"Sort of like birds," he said. "Thousands of sharks in packs so large they look like black clouds in video shot from airplanes. Most people are afraid to go in the water during the migration. I'm not saying it's safe, but if you spend enough time on a boat, you'll learn that sharks—especially blacktips—eat fish, not people. On the rare occasion a person's bitten, it's not an attack. It's an accident—a case of mistaken identity."

In the shallow water around the island, he explained, blacktips are seldom bigger than a few feet long and rarely weigh more than twenty pounds. People are much too large for them to eat. Blacktips feed on small sea creatures such as fish and crabs.

Sabina, seated next to Maribel, joked quietly, "That explains why *mamá* told me not to be crabby this morning."

Luke reacted with a momentary smile. It was the first sign of emotion from the boy, the sisters noticed.

Not all blacktips migrate north in the summer, the biologist continued. The female sharks often winter in the bays between Tampa and Key West. They give birth to their young in the spring. It is usually male blacktip sharks, not the females, that gather in schools of thousands. They travel north or south together, depending on the season.

"What some scientists are worried about," Dr. Ford explained, "is video shot during the last few years that suggests fewer blacktips are making the trip. The question is, are they staying in the bays along south Florida? Or are there fewer sharks?"

Shark populations worldwide, he added, were in trouble for many reasons. But the main reason was sad and simple.

"Shark-fin soup," he said. "It's considered a delicacy, which is why some countries have banned it from menus. But many have not. The fins sell for a lot of money—several hundred dollars a pound. It takes a bunch of shark fins to equal a pound, and the saddest thing is that's all they use—the fins. They throw the rest of the fish away. Some people suspect the blacktips are being netted during their migration. Others believe that the water temperature is rising, so those fish have no need to migrate. There's no way to know unless we can track the sharks. That's why tagging is important."

He opened a box of tiny plastic tags—spaghetti tags,

they were called. They were an inch long. At one end was a metal dart. At the other end was a thread stamped with a number. Each came with a card that had to be filled out. This was to be done after the shark had been tagged and released into the wild.

Later, the information and a photo of the shark would be uploaded to an international database.

"There's a procedure," he said. "It has to be done exactly right every time. Sharks can be tagged without hurting them or getting hurt yourself. That's what we're going to practice for the next few days. Convince me you can do the job, and do it safely, *then* we'll discuss the three of you using a rental boat."

"Alone? Just us?" Luke asked.

The man nodded. "That's what this program is all about—kids your age learning by actually doing. It'll be fun, but it's also serious work. And remember: If that day comes, you can't fish anywhere but inside this bay. Ever. Understood?"

They were in Dinkins Bay. It was a small salty lake encircled by rubbery trees called mangroves. The marina—Dinkins Bay Marina—and the biologist's lab were visible onshore a mile away.

Mangroves, Luke thought. He attempted to memorize the word even though he had never seen uglier trees in his life. They were nothing like the forests of oak and maple in the farming region west of Toledo. Mangroves were more like bushes buzzed flat by the wind. They clustered together in hedges of green and dropped roots in the shallows. The tangled roots resembled coils of barbed wire. Or toothy wooden spikes that surrounded the islands they protected.

The boy had to admit, however, that mangroves were home to more nesting birds than he'd ever seen. Clumsy brown pelicans with quivering neck sacks, and oil-black birds with green lizard eyes. These and many other birds watched the biologist rig two heavy fishing rods.

"The black birds are cormorants," Dr. Ford said. "They dive and swim underwater. In Asia, fishermen train them to catch fish and return to the boat. Don't get your hands near one of our local cormorants, though. They're not as sociable here."

The biologist chuckled while Luke repeated the name silently to himself. *Cor-mor-ant.*

Maybe he would remember these new words. Maybe he wouldn't. One thing he felt sure of was that something inside his head had changed. Since the thunderstorm, there had been days when his memory was as sharp and bright as the lightning bolt that had left scars on his body. On other occasions, though, his brain was just as foggy as it had been back on the farm. This was frustrating. True, he had never taken the trouble to try to remember difficult words before. Why make the effort? He wasn't the sharpest hook in the box, as he'd been told many times.

But now, after being struck by lightning, maybe that had changed.

Dr. Ford broke into his thoughts, saying, "Because we don't want to injure the sharks, we'll use special hooks. See?" He held up a fishhook that was larger than the hooks Luke had used to snatch catfish from the pond, but otherwise the same.

No, they weren't the same, the biologist informed him.

"These hooks are barbless—easy to remove from a fish's mouth. And they're made of wire that will bend if you hook something too big to handle. Or they'll dissolve after a week or so if the line breaks. We're not fishing for food. This is research, not a sport, so we're using heavy line and rods. If a shark takes the bait, we want to get it to the boat, tag it, and release it as fast as possible."

"If there *are* any sharks," Sabina said, looking up from the book she'd brought along. The girl was already getting bored.

Behind the boat, seagulls soared in the sleepy heat. The chum slick drifted from the entrance of the bay into a larger body of water called Pine Island Sound. Water out there was deeper, open to the wind.

A couple of miles away, around a sandy stretch of beach, was Woodring's Point and the Gulf of Mexico. The Gulf was a vast desert of blue, where a boat might drift hundreds of miles before reaching Mexico. Or Cuba, two hundred miles to the south.

"Patience, young lady," the biologist said. He baited a hook, cast it off the back of the boat, and placed the rod in a holder next to Sabina.

"The first shark that hits is yours," he warned. "Be ready."

FOUR
A MONSTER SHARK

The hour they spent waiting for sharks to appear was like being in an outdoor classroom—but a lot more fun. The biologist was quizzing them on the dangers of removing saltwater catfish from a hook when Luke suddenly got to his feet. "Holy moly," he murmured.

It was because of what he saw: Something long and dark was snaking toward them beneath water that was blue-green but not clear.

"Speak English," Sabina snapped, looking up from her book.

"I am," Luke said. "What the heck is that thing?"

The biologist shaded his eyes. "I'm not sure what you mean. I don't see anything. Maribel, what about you?"

"Maybe," she replied. She didn't want to embarrass a boy who was new to saltwater fishing. "Could've been a cloud passing over. Or a bird, I guess."

A squadron of seagulls had assembled above the chum slick, diving and squawking and battling over bits of fish.

Sabina returned to her book. "What do you expect from a farm boy who doesn't know squat? He's imagining things."

"Mind your tongue," Maribel said. At the same time, Dr. Ford asked Luke, "How far?"

"The thing I see?" Luke aimed a gloved finger and said, "Quite a ways."

"Give me an estimate in yards."

Maribel watched the boy turn inward as if consulting a secret source of information. "Um . . . about the same distance from home plate to second base," he said. "No . . . now it's closer. Whatever it is, it's big. Couldn't be a shark, could it?"

"Home to second base." The biologist liked the comparison but wasn't particularly excited. "You must play baseball. Are you a catcher?

"Sometimes. When I don't have to work."

"That's a wise approach. Always reference what you know. But . . . I still don't see what you see."

"The shadow of a cloud," Maribel suggested again, and looked up.

There were no clouds.

The biologist searched for a while longer, then took a seat. "The light's tricky out here," he said. "It takes a while to train your eyes to notice changes on the surface. You'll learn to look *through* the water to understand what you're seeing. Don't get discouraged."

The dark shape had a tail curved into a point. It fanned mud off the bottom as the creature moved. Luke's heart was pounding. He spoke softly to Maribel. "That thing—whatever it is—is swimming straight at your sister's line. Tell her to put the book away."

Sabina responded, "Tell me yourself. I don't take orders from her."

The girl sat back as if bored, then dropped the book, startled, when water exploded behind the boat. The rod she was tending bent with a sudden strain like it had snagged a passing motorcycle. The reel shrieked. Line was being stripped off by whatever had taken the bait.

"What happened?!" she yelled.

"You've got a fish on," the biologist said calmly. "Leave the rod in the rod holder. That fish is too big. Hopefully, the hook will bend free, and it'll get off."

"But it's my fish," the girl argued.

"Too big," the man said again. "If you can't follow the rules, you can't tag sharks." He forced a stern look that caused Maribel to hide a smile behind her hand.

"It's turning this way again," Luke said. He'd barely blinked since he'd spotted the creature that moved like a large swimming snake. "It's coming back toward the boat. If it was a shark, wouldn't I see a fin?"

That's the way it always was in movies.

"Seldom" was the reply. Dr. Ford studied the boy for a moment. "I'll be darned. You were right—you did see something, and it wasn't a cloud. Luke, your eyesight is unusual . . . extraordinary, even." He turned to Sabina. "Leave the rod in the holder and start reeling in slack."

"Slack?" the girl shouted. "What does that mean? Doesn't anyone speak Spanish anymore?"

"Sit next to the rod and crank in line before it gets tangled," the man instructed. When Maribel gave him a *Should I help her?* look, he shook his head. "She can do it."

Sabina flashed her sister a wicked grin and proved the biologist right by reeling furiously.

Behind her, Luke whispered in awe, "Holy moly—look at the size of that thing. It's a monster."

The dark shape was so close they could all see it now. It had a massive blunt head and fins like wings. It was longer than the boat was wide.

"A bull shark," Dr. Ford said. "A big one. Maribel, get the camera and start taking pictures. Luke, keep your gloves on just in case. I'll rig the tag pole. Who knows—if it comes close enough, we might get lucky and stick a tag in it."

Hurrying to ready the equipment, he reminded them, "Hands in the boat. And no leaning over the side."

When Sabina got her first look at the shark, her mouth dropped open. She muttered a single harsh word in Spanish.

"No curse words," scolded Maribel. "Keep reeling. Luke, move out of my way and get a tag ready for Dr. Ford." The older girl was already familiar with the little waterproof camera. She began snapping shots, then switched to video. The viewfinder brought what happened next into sharp focus.

The bull shark, as if unaware of the hook in its mouth,

glided slowly toward the boat. Its triangular dorsal fin pierced the surface for the first time. The creature had a broad, gray back. Clinging to it were several smaller fish that had hitched a ride. The size and shape of the shark, and the way it used its tail like a rudder, reminded her of a small submarine.

The biologist appeared in the camera's viewfinder. He held a pole that resembled a broom handle. The point was sharp as a needle.

"Sabina, it's your fish," he said. "If it gets close enough, you're going to help me tag it. Luke, watch the line for tangles—especially if it gets tangled around you or one of the girls. If that happens, cut the line. Maribel, watch everything. As of now, you're in charge of the boat."

In charge?

The older sister lowered the camera for a moment. "What do you want me to do?"

"Whatever you think needs to be done," the man replied. He said it in a way that meant she really was in charge.

The shark, still on the line, nosed closer to the chum bag near the motor, then sunk out of sight. For several seconds no one spoke.

"There it is," Luke said, pointing again.

A moment later, the bull shark surfaced beside the boat. It was close enough that Maribel could have touched its tail if she hadn't resumed shooting video.

"*Now*," the biologist said.

With Sabina's hand on the pole, in a single jab, he inserted a tag behind the shark's dorsal fin. The needle made a crunching sound when it pierced the rough skin. Again, the water exploded. The rod buckled with the shark's weight . . . then the fish was gone.

"The hook bent," Luke said when he'd reeled in the line. "Just like you said." He held up the straightened hook for them all to see.

"Excellent job, guys, all of you." The biologist was grinning. "Teamwork, that's what shark tagging is all about. I'm impressed." After sharing some high fives, he became serious. "Big sharks are rare in this bay, so it probably won't happen again. But you will never try to tag an animal that size. Understood? You'll leave the rod in the rod holder and tighten the drag until it breaks free. I'll show you how."

They all nodded. Maribel began to fill out a data card that matched the number on the tag they'd inserted behind the dorsal fin. The tag would accompany the monster shark wherever it traveled.

"Filling out the card is the shark tagger's job," Dr. Ford informed the older sister with a sly smile. "And, Sabina? Write in English or Spanish—it's up to you. This is an international research project."

FIVE
THE FIRST SHARK, A POEM, AND A BROKEN POLE

Every day that week the three children fished in the bay as a team. The biologist, or Luke's aunt, Captain Hannah Smith, observed. On a Monday afternoon, Maribel caught, measured, and tagged their first blacktip shark. It was twenty-eight inches long—small enough to hold in her hands before gently inserting a tag beneath its gritty sandpaper skin.

By their fifth trip, they had tagged and released fourteen small sharks, most of them blacktips. They were learning to work together as a team. Everyone had an assigned task. They took turns reeling in the fish, or shooting video, or readying a new tag. It felt like a game, yet they all knew it wasn't. They were getting good at what Dr. Ford called the *tagging procedure*.

"Sharks Incorporated," Captain Hannah joked after another long day on the water. It was obvious the woman appreciated their enthusiasm and businesslike attitudes.

Maribel liked the name. When they were alone, she wondered if they could have T-shirts made. "Nice ones," she suggested, "just for the three of us, plus a couple of adult sizes for Hannah and Dr. Ford."

Luke didn't have an opinion.

That irritated Sabina, who was busy cleaning the boat. All week the farm boy had been like this. With no adults around, why didn't he share her mild sense of relief? It was their chance to talk and laugh and say whatever they wanted without being polite. Instead, he got even quieter.

It wasn't the boy's reluctance to talk that irked her. It was the odd confidence his silence suggested. It was as if he knew things he wasn't willing to share. More annoying was that when Maribel spoke, Luke paid attention. But when she, Sabina, said something, he seemed to ignore her.

Sabina didn't like being snubbed—especially by a boy who, to her, was strange enough to be sort of interesting. She sloshed a scrub brush in a bucket of suds and looked up at Luke. He was futzing with a broken shark-tagging pole that was actually an old broom handle. "You might like Cuba," she said in a friendly way. "Since you don't speak Spanish, no one would understand you, even if you did have something to say. There'd be no need to talk at all. Wouldn't that be nice?"

The boy swatted at a mosquito near his ear but might as well have been swatting the question away. The cracked broom handle had his full attention.

Sabina exchanged looks with Maribel. The older sister was separating trash for the recycle bins. "Maybe he's not interested in getting T-shirts," she said. "Besides, I think Luke would like Cuba. Everybody plays baseball on the island. Boys, girls, everybody."

The farm boy was suddenly interested. "Baseball? You play? What position?"

That began a conversation—their first with no adults around. Maribel said she preferred the infield, but mostly she played soccer. In the village where they'd lived, miles from Havana, kids couldn't afford baseball equipment. But one soccer ball was enough to keep everyone happy.

"What we did," she explained, "was find a piece of wood and carve it into a bat. For baseballs, you know that black stuff they put on roads that melts when the sun's hot?" She couldn't think of the word in English.

"*Asfalto,*" Sabina suggested in Spanish.

"Asphalt?" Luke asked. "Like tar?"

"Yes, to make baseballs," Maribel said. "Wait for a hot afternoon. You get a glob about the size of a golf ball and roll it in your hands. Sorta like clay. Then you wrap it round and round with string until it's big enough. That takes a lot of string, so sometimes we used fishing line. Next, some electrical tape as a cover, but that was hard to find, too."

"Come on—kids make their own bats and balls?" Luke wondered if Maribel was pranking him. No . . . it was true. He could tell by her mannerisms, the easygoing way she spoke. "That's kinda cool, I guess. I never thought about making my own bat."

They talked about it while they finished their work. What kind of wood did the Cuban kids use? And what about catcher's gear, shin guards and a mask?

Sabina demonstrated. She made a mask with her right hand by pressing five fingers to her face. "The kids dumb enough to be catchers do this," she said. She squatted, peeking through her fingers, and extended her left hand as if about to catch a pitch.

The boy actually grinned. "You've got to be kidding. No mask, just a bare hand?" His grin faded when Sabina lifted her front lip. There was a gap there, and her lip showed a pale scar.

"How do you think I lost my tooth?" she said. "Not that I care. It'll grow back."

"You're a"—Luke was trying to picture it—"you're a catcher?"

"Someone has to tell the pitcher what to do," Sabina said, done with the subject of baseball. "I gave up stupid games, though. Now I write poetry. Do you like poetry?" She stored the scrub brush and stepped onto the dock.

"You write poems even if a teacher doesn't make you?" For Luke, the concept was even harder to grasp than the idea of a ten-year-old catcher without a face mask. "That can't be any fun."

The girl grimaced as if offended. "Poetry isn't supposed to be fun. It's about love and sadness and being poor—too poor to buy new shoes or even an iPhone. In Havana, there is the most beautiful cemetery in the world. Huge, a forest of beautiful stone. My favorite poet, Dulce María Borrero, is buried there. I would take flowers to her grave and eat a sandwich. Would you like to hear one of her poems? I memorized two of them in English."

"Maybe later," Luke said. He eyed the cracked tagging pole as he asked, "Do they rhyme?"

"What's it matter if you don't want to hear them?" the girl responded. "My poems, I like them to rhyme, but poems don't have to rhyme. I don't think you know squat about poetry, either."

Maribel, sensing an argument felt a familiar tension in her stomach. She tried to get back to the T-shirts. "Sabina is the artistic one. Together, maybe we could design something nice. 'Sharks Incorporated,' what do you think?"

For a moment the boy was interested. He started to say, "I can talk to my aunt about it . . ." But then his attention shifted. His gaze focused on a distant shoreline where mangroves shaded the water.

"I gotta go," he muttered. "Pete's up to no good."

"Pete?" Maribel replied. "Oh, the dog."

Luke scooped up the tagging pole, and got a gloved hand on a tackle box. "He's been chewing the ropes off boats and towing them out into the bay. Boat owners think they're stolen."

Sabina followed the boy's gaze. "I don't see anything.

You're making that up." As he walked away, she added, "Hey—you're just trying to get out of hearing a beautiful poem. Or mad because I've caught more sharks than you."

"I think I might make a new tagging pole," Luke replied, his mind somewhere far off.

It was true that, so far, Sabina had been the luckiest fisherman of them all. She had landed nine of the fourteen sharks they'd tagged that week. In her diary, days ago, she had described the blacktip sharks as *magníficos*. The fish were silver and black. They were as sleek as rockets, and their eyes resembled those of a fierce cat. Or a meanhearted goat.

In Cuba, both animals were common.

Thinking about her former home always caused a bout of melancholy in the girl. A few days earlier, alone in the little houseboat where she lived with her mother and sister, Sabina had written a poem entitled "Gatos con Cuernos."

"Cats with Horns" was the title after she had laboriously translated it into English. She had done some editing to make the unfamiliar English words rhyme, then folded the poem and placed it in a secret drawer in her desk.

Today, after talking about Havana's beautiful cemetery and her favorite poet, Sabina felt melancholy descend on her on like a cloud. Luke had snubbed her again. Maribel, of course, had taken his side. Not that Sabina cared—not really—but the boy had to be an airhead not to like poetry.

Alone, she walked to their small blue-and-white houseboat moored at the end of the dock. The space it had been assigned was far from where the bigger, shinier, more expensive boats were tied. A gate on the houseboat railing allowed the girl onto the well-scrubbed deck. Flowers grew there in pots along the outside wall of what was her family's new home.

"*¿Mamá?*" she said, stepping inside, and was relieved to confirm that her mother was at work. Sabina often craved solitude. She hurried down the hall to her room and bolted the door. The room was tiny. It contained a single bed, a narrow desk, and a closet behind a curtain. Here her mind could roam privately to any place in the world she wanted to go.

She sat at the desk and opened a drawer that contained her private possessions. Inside was her diary, a candle, and a miniature doll made of woven straw. There were also strings of blue and yellow beads from her favorite shop in Havana. She had loved slipping off by herself to visit that shop. It smelled of cinnamon and incense, and the women in white—priestesses some called them—had treated Sabina as one of their own.

Also in the desk was a poem she had written the previous day. It was about Luke. Secretly, the farm boy's moody silences, and his unusual eyesight, had impressed Sabina in a way that gave her an odd feeling in her stomach. Now she was tempted to tear up the stupid poem and throw it away.

She nearly did. She crumpled the paper into a ball. She hurled it across the room, then ignored it by opening her diary. But Sabina couldn't concentrate. Words written on paper, as the women in white had explained, possessed a spirit and a power of their own.

After a while, the girl gave up. She retrieved the paper and freed the words by lighting a candle and then smoothing the paper flat on her desk.

Translated, the poem read:

> *A boy who sees what cannot be seen*
> *Who hears words unspoken*

A boy even stranger than me
Who doesn't know squat
And is dumb as a rock
Although my sister would not agree

On the boat ride home, Captain Hannah said to Luke, "You take the controls. I think Izaak is hungry."

It was late afternoon. The bay was calm, a waxen green.

The woman sat with her back to him, holding the baby. Luke stood at the wheel and steered toward a distant point of land. A clearing in the mangroves showed a clutter of docks. Houses there were elevated above the water on what locals called "Indian mounds." They were ancient hills built of shells thousands of years ago by Florida's First People.

Hannah's boat was sleeker and faster than the clunky rental boat Luke and the sisters had been using. It gave the boy a good feeling to know his aunt trusted him to drive. He liked the way the deck felt beneath his feet, the way the hull sliced through waves. It reminded him of driving a snowmobile—neighbors had owned one back in Ohio. But the Florida air was warm. It smelled of salt and iodine and did not sting when breathed in.

When they were close to the fishing village where Hannah and Luke's grandpa lived, Hannah said, "Good job. I'd let you dock the boat, but it's getting late." Then she noticed the broom handle that was Dr. Ford's shark-tagging pole among Luke's things. "Why'd you bring that?"

"There's a crack near the point. Figured I'd fix it, because I'm the one who broke it. The tagging stick we usually use is a lot smaller, so we can get along without this one for a while."

His aunt wasn't the talkative type when she was driving a boat. "Marion likes you. He'll appreciate that" is all she said.

Luke's Grandfather Futch *was* the talkative type, no matter where or what time of day. Some of the strange things the old man said puzzled the boy yet often made him smile. Like now. They were in the kitchen. It was a crowded space with a propane stove, a sink, and a refrigerator that was probably as old as the fishing captain.

"Raised pigs in 4-H, did you?" Grandpa Futch asked. He was frying potatoes in a skillet while Luke set the table for three. Hannah and baby Izaak would be joining them for dinner.

"A couple of black Angus cattle, too," Luke said. "Mind if I excuse myself after I get the baby's chair set up? I need to look for something while it's still light. I broke our shark-tagging pole today, and I need to fix it."

"You raised cattle?" The old man sneered, more interested in black Angus than the tagging pole. "Cows aren't good for nothing but milk and mooing. Give me a pig any day."

"Pigs are cool," Luke agreed, but wanted to stay on topic. "Did you hear what I said about breaking that pole? I need to find the right piece of wood. It belongs to Dr. Ford."

"Son," the old man said, "I'm trying to teach you something here about being a sea captain. If your boat starts to sink—you can be a thousand miles offshore, it don't matter—and if you're carrying a cargo of livestock, the first thing you do is find the pigs. Pigs are *smart*. You can drop a pig in the middle of an ocean at midnight, and he'll swim straight for land. It's a gift that pigs are born with. Only the good Lord knows why."

Luke found this educational but was determined to get

outside. "I'd like to use the toolshed, if it's okay. Maribel—she's one of the girls I mentioned—she told me that kids in Cuba make their own baseball bats. That gave me an idea. I'm gonna made a brand-new tagging pole."

His grandfather seemed not to hear. "Take a cow or a horse—never depend on those animals for directions. Sheep and goats are almost as bad. Now, a dog—heck, a dog will chase seagulls, it don't matter to him. A dog could swim forty miles of open water and just be touching the beach—but if a seagull flies over? Forget it. A dang dog will head right back out to sea."

"You don't like dogs?" Luke asked. That was disappointing news.

"Not in this house," the old man said. "Never again. Last dog we had 'bout got me ate up with fleas." With a fork, he flipped the potatoes in a cast-iron skillet. Grease sputtered. "But a cat"—his grandfather reached for a mug of coffee—"now, there's an animal worth knowing. A cat's got brains. Know how you can tell? That's right—if your boat sinks, a cat will already be in the water, waiting to climb onto the first pig that swims past."

Luke consulted the nearest window. The sun was down, but the sky was still golden with light. He also noticed the oak tree that had been splintered by lightning on the same afternoon he'd been zapped.

"How long before we eat?" he asked.

"A lot faster than it will take you to carve a baseball bat" was the response.

Apparently, his grandfather had been listening.

"Not a bat," Luke said. "A new tagging pole. It'll take me a couple of days to finish it the way I want."

"Okay, but be back here in thirty minutes," the old man said. He waited until the boy was at the screen door to add, "You're good at fixing things, I'll say that much for you. Folks put way too much stock in being smart. I'll take a hard worker any day."

The boy took that as a compliment. "Thanks. Can I use the lathe?" A lathe was a machine with spindles that rotated. It had a cutting blade in the middle.

"Most kids, I'd say no"—his grandfather took a sip from the coffee mug—"but you're pretty good with tools, too. There're plenty of wood scraps in the shed. Help yourself."

Luke had a different piece of wood in mind.

SIX

IF A SHARK JUMPS INTO THE BOAT

On days the three children didn't fish, there was a short classroom session, usually outdoors. Dr. Ford wasn't always around. Some days, he would leave alone on his boat. Other days, he flew off in the pretty blue-and-white seaplane he kept on a floating dock tethered in the mangroves.

On those occasions, Captain Hannah was in charge. She led them in safety drills, using one of the rental boats. They learned to row the boat using heavy wooden oars. Another useful skill was knowing how to drain water from the boat in a hurry by pulling a plug beneath the engine and using the throttle to speed ahead.

Hannah also made up flash cards that had to do with fishing and boating safety. The cards were used, rapid-fire, in daily pop quizzes. The kids sometimes borrowed the cards or quizzed one another from memory.

How do you tell the difference between a blacktip shark and a spinner shark? was one of the questions. The two fish were almost identical in appearance.

The answer: A spinner shark has a small black fin beneath its tail—an anal fin, it's called. Blacktip sharks have whitish anal fins, but the tip of their dorsal fin is jet black.

There were many flash cards, and many more questions.

What's the difference between a bull shark and a sandbar shark? Very few fishermen know.

A bull shark has a blunt nose and no rough-looking ridge on its back. A sandbar shark has a visible ridge on its back. Its dorsal fin is taller and broader.

Why are saltwater catfish and stingrays more dangerous than sharks?

This had seemed an absurd question that couldn't possibly be true. But it was true. Saltwater catfish and stingrays are both equipped with needlelike spines that can pierce a person's hands or feet. The spines inject a protein venom that isn't deadly but requires immediate first aid. Hot water—as hot as the victim can stand—and a good scrubbing with antiseptic are necessary, then a trip to a doctor just to be safe.

What should you do if a shark jumps into the boat?

This wasn't a silly question, either. Blacktips and spinner sharks often jump high out of the water, especially on the end of a hook.

Answer: Don't panic—that is the most important thing. Wait for the shark to calm down, then cover it with a towel. When safe, tag the shark and revive it in the water.

What are two of the most common causes of serious boating accidents?

This embarrassing question was posed several times by a very serious Captain Hannah.

The answer: The cause of most accidents, for men, is urinating over the side while the motor is running. For men and women, it is losing a hat in a speeding boat, then circling back to retrieve the hat. Both scenarios cause people to lose their balance and fall overboard where a spinning propeller might kill them—and often does.

This inspired Luke, who still didn't say much, to address an awkward topic. "What if I have to . . . you know, *go*, while we're out there on the water, just me and two girls? Or if they have to, you know, use the bathroom, what should we do?"

Answer: Stop the boat, shut off the engine, and use a bucket while all passengers face forward.

"Sometimes music helps," Captain Hannah suggested in a fun way. "Turn it loud and relax until the person using the bucket turns the music off. That's the signal they're done."

Maribel liked Hannah. On Friday, the woman spent an hour with the trio in a rental boat. They didn't fish, just focused on safety issues. She had entrusted the care of her child, baby Izaak, to the biologist and his dog.

In Maribel's mind, this and some other clues partly explained why Dr. Ford was spending so much time helping three local kids learn to tag sharks and work around his laboratory.

It was his excuse to see Hannah and the baby. But there was another reason, Maribel suspected. It was also a way to keep an eye on Luke at the request of his aunt, the fishing guide. This suggested that the boy was recovering from an illness or was somehow different from other kids.

Maybe he was.

Maribel had seen the biologist focus on the boy as if studying him through a microscope. *Studying* seemed the correct word.

It was hard to understand why, at times, Luke had trouble remembering even the simplest things. He would wander off in a daze, then return as if he'd just awakened from a dream. When that happened, he could sometimes glance at a flash card and recite every line *exactly* as it was written.

Dr. Ford seemed more mystified by Luke's unusual eyesight. How had the boy seen the monster bull shark before anyone else did? How had he known the shark would surface beside the boat while it was still deep underwater?

Something else strange was the retriever's behavior. Dr. Ford had been the only person in the world whom that dog obeyed—until Luke appeared. The boy didn't even have to speak. He would just motion, or mouth a command—sit, stay, come, heel—and the dog responded immediately.

"He communicates with animals through the air," her sister, the secret witch, claimed. Then sounded a tad jealous when she added, "I don't know why you talk about Luke so much, Maribel. He can do what he does because he grew up on a farm with filthy pigs and other animals no smarter than him."

A mystery Sabina could not explain was why Luke almost always wore gloves. On the rare occasions he took them off, Maribel paid close attention. The boy had thick, hard hands. They reminded her of the hands of sugar-cane workers in Cuba, although his skin was many shades lighter than theirs. His hair was reddish blond, and his right hand was usually curled into a fist.

Was he hiding something?

"The answer is simple. Tell him I'm a palm reader," Sabina suggested that afternoon when Hannah and Luke were gone. "I can tell his future if he'll open his big, ugly hands."

"Dr. Ford will think we're weird," Maribel responded.

Her little sister didn't care. "Everyone thinks I'm weird. So what?"

Maribel cared. "The man's a scientist, and scientists laugh at magic tricks."

"If it was any other scientist," Sabina said, "I'd place a hex on him and wipe the smile off his face. I can do it. The women in white taught me. You and *mamá* never found out where I went those times I pretended to get lost in Havana."

Without thinking, the girl's fingers found the blue and yellow beads around her neck.

Maribel knew about the spooky store her sister had visited whenever she could sneak away. But why cause trouble by admitting it?

"Dr. Ford will think we're *locas*," Maribel insisted.

Sabina was even more stubborn than Pete, the curly-haired dog, so Maribel had to compromise. "If you're going to trick Luke by pretending to be palm reader, at least wait until they let the three of us tag sharks alone. Next week, perhaps."

"Next year, more like it," Sabina grumbled. "They'll never trust three kids our age alone in a boat."

Over the weekend, Maribel fretted about her sister's prediction. Captain Hannah had fishing charters. The biologist was busy, or away on a trip, so there would be no shark tagging until Monday at the earliest.

It gave the girl lots of time to worry. Had she, her sister, and Luke somehow failed to prove themselves worthy? If so, the problem wasn't Luke. The boy never complained. Although sometimes absentminded, he could see and hear things on the water that even adults could not. And Sabina was incredibly lucky when it came to catching sharks.

Saturday night, Maribel lay awake while an inner voice nagged and made sleep impossible. It accused her of being the reason they would never be trusted alone in the rental boat. *The problem is you, not them*, the voice taunted. *Why don't you say more, do more? You should work harder, Maribel. Why aren't you brave enough to speak out like Sabina?*

On Sunday morning, Maribel's mother noticed dark circles under the girl's eyes. "*Mi pequeña general*," the woman said in Spanish. "My little general"—it was the nickname she'd given Maribel as a child. "You've always carried the weight of the world on your shoulders. What's wrong, my dear? Didn't you sleep?"

Her mother, Marta Estéban, dressed like a housemaid but had the elegant face of an Aztec princess. On the internet, in videos of lost cities in the jungle, there were similar faces carved in stone.

"I know what's troubling you," the woman continued. "You have to deal with paperwork when you should be out having fun." She indicated a stack of new bills on the kitchen counter. "Don't let them upset you, my darling.

Compared to the bad things we survived in Cuba, they are nothing. We'll manage. We always do."

Maribel wasn't so sure. When her mother was gone, she sat and opened the bills one by one. On the table was a ledger they'd bought at Bailey's General Store. Since moving into the houseboat, Maribel had done the bookkeeping. She knew, better than her mother did, how tight money was.

The girl made entries with a pencil, always. It was easier to erase, and pausing to use the electric pencil sharpener provided a nice break. The clean, precise point the machine created, time after time, was calming.

A pencil, no matter how dull, could be made new again.

This week's bills weren't too bad. The girl added, and subtracted, and tallied the little blocks at the bottom of the ledger. Done, she stood and took pride in the neatness of her work before closing the book.

Maybe her mother was right. In Cuba, a terrifying series of events had forced them to flee to Florida. There had been a hurricane. Lightning had burned their little thatched house. They'd gone without food, and Sabina had angered a bad man who'd come with soldiers and guns.

Compared to all this, money meant nothing. In fact,

a bundle of new bills was no worse than a shark jumping into the boat, Maribel decided. Don't panic, stay calm. They would find a way to manage.

The girl felt better after that. And when her inner voice attempted to ruin this beautiful summer morning, she dealt with it in a new way. She pictured a small shark leaping into the rental boat. Could see the poor thing flopping around until it was covered by a towel, then safely released. The scene that played out in her head was sort of funny. There was no danger. Not really. The danger, like the inner voice that taunted her, was imaginary.

Maribel smiled, walking to the kitchen. Her sister always slept late on Sundays. Sabina would want breakfast before they had to dress for church. In the fridge was a fresh mango, eggs, a wedge of salty goat cheese. There was also a thick slice of carrot cake from the restaurant where their mother worked as a server.

Maribel put on music—a soft mambo by Celia Cruz. The girl danced as she often did while she worked. *Secretly.*

SEVEN
SHARKS INCORPORATED!

On Monday morning, Luke stepped off Captain Hannah's boat and joined the sisters. They were sitting in the shade beneath the biologist's house, which they all referred to as "the lab."

"My aunt has something she wants to give you," the boy said. He was more interested in the dog sprinting toward them.

"What? Another test?" Sabina asked. "I'm sick of tests. They make my brain tired."

"Don't be so negative," Maribel said gently. She was no longer troubled by thoughts of failure. But she was hungry, so she added, "Maybe she brought us something good to eat."

Hannah made excellent jelly from wild sea grapes that

grew on the islands. Sometimes she brought fragrant smoked mullet—an odd-looking type of fish. Or a pot of pinto beans, or a stalk of sweet bananas. The woman had even surprised them with ice cream flavored with wild oranges and a coconut she had milked and grated herself.

"That would be nice," Sabina agreed. "Those tests make me hungry, too. I don't suppose your aunt knows where a wild chocolate tree grows? I like chocolate better than coconut. In Cuba, I drank so much coconut water I got sick once."

Luke ignored her.

He said to the dog, "*Pete . . . heel,*" and they trotted off together toward the steps that led up to the laboratory. "She wants Dr. Ford to be here when you open the package," he informed the sisters with a backward glance. "But he wants to talk to me about something first."

"A *package,*" Sabina said. She was intrigued.

Captain Hannah appeared on the path to the lab. She wore a long-sleeved khaki shirt as protection from the sun and was carrying baby Izaak in a sling. In her free hand was a large sack.

"Don't spoil the surprise by asking what she brought us," Maribel whispered.

Her sister nodded. But when the woman was closer,

Sabina asked, "Want me to carry that sack? It looks heavy. What's in it?"

Hannah touched a finger to her lips in a secretive way. "Be right back," she said. "Get ready for a quick pop quiz on you-know-what."

"I don't want to know what," Sabina complained after the door to the lab had banged shut. But sat up straight when the woman returned ten minutes later, carrying only the sack—and the flash cards, of course. This meant another test.

"Pretend you're the skipper of a boat," Captain Hannah instructed. "Don't bother to raise your hand to answer. On the water, bad things happen fast, and you don't have time to be polite. You have to act immediately. And to follow orders, no matter who's in charge. Ready?"

"Where's Luke?" Sabina asked.

"With Marion," Hannah said. She sometimes called the biologist by his first name. More often, she referred to him as "Doc."

Sabina wasn't satisfied. "If we have to take a test, why doesn't Luke?"

"He passed the test on the boat ride here," the woman responded patiently. "Ready? Okay, here we go."

The questioning began, rapid-fire.

When is the only time you don't have to wear your PFDs?

PFD stood for "personal flotation device," or life vest. She was referring to the inflatable suspenders they had learned how to adjust and use.

Answer: Only on calm days, when the boat was at anchor, were they allowed to take off their PFDs.

"When you're driving a boat," Hannah continued, "what's the first thing you should do if your engine quits unexpectedly?"

The answer was: Wait until the boat slows, then drop the anchor to keep the boat from drifting into a dangerous situation.

What do you do if your boat hits a sandbar?

Answer: Shut off the engine immediately. Tilt the propeller out of the water and get the anchor ready in case the boat drifts free.

When there are storm clouds in the area, what does it mean when the wind suddenly shifts and the air feels cooler?

Answer: Return to the marina immediately. A storm is coming your way.

Captain Hannah became serious when discussing

bad weather. In Florida, thunderheads brought rain almost every summer afternoon. Lightning was a killer, the woman said, as she had many times before.

The quiz about safety went on for a while: *What do you do if a passenger falls overboard? Loses a hat? What if the boat starts leaking water? If the engine catches fire? What is the emergency code word if a boater needs immediate* help?—MAYDAY!

Then there was a trick question. "Let's say you're off Woodring's Point in the Gulf of Mexico. Your anchor line breaks in a heavy wind, and you begin to drift out of sight of land. What do you do?"

Sabina replied, "I would teach Luke more Spanish. That farm boy will need it if we all don't drown before we reach Mexico."

"Not a bad answer," Hannah said, smiling, "but it's not what I was hoping to hear."

"We're not allowed to fish outside this bay," Maribel reminded Sabina, which earned a glare from her sister. "We'll never be in the Gulf."

The fishing guide nodded her approval. "Never out of sight of the lab or the marina. Those are the rules. And if you need help, what do you do?"

In the rental boat was a set of oars, a flare gun, a red towel, and a small handheld marine radio.

"First try calling on the radio," Maribel answered. "If that doesn't work, tie the towel to an oar and wave it to get someone's attention. If that doesn't work, fire the flare gun—it's dangerous, but we've all learned to use it."

"Good," Hannah said. She pointed to the lab's upper deck. "And if someone raises a red flag on that pole?"

"Return to the marina immediately," Maribel responded. "It probably has to do with a lightning storm, but it could be something else important."

After a glance at the youngest sister, the fishing guide asked a final question. "If one of your crew refuses to wear a life vest or argues about their job, what have you been instructed to do?"

Sabina replied, "I know, I know. Order me to sit down and take me straight back to the marina. Don't worry. If anyone breaks the rules, it'll be Luke or Maribel. Not me."

The woman applauded and said "Excellent" before checking her watch. "Let's give Luke and Doc another few minutes. I've got a surprise for you."

After a while, though, the fishing guide changed her mind. "What the heck. I want to see the look on Luke's face when he comes down those steps. Put these on if you like them."

From the sack, she removed three long-billed fishing caps. Next came three good-looking, navy blue T-shirts.

"Hold one up," Hannah said, "and see what's written on the front. I had them made just for you."

On the front of the shirts, bold gold letters read:

SHARKS INCORPORATED
Research Team Member

Luke was unaware of what was going on outside. He was studying the aquariums that lined the wall of the laboratory. They housed many types of local fish and crabs, even seahorses. In the last couple of weeks, he'd learned how to care for these glass tanks that bubbled with life. He was also trying to memorize the names of the less obvious creatures that lived on the bottom of the tanks. Dr. Ford said it was part of his job.

It wasn't easy.

Some were animals that looked like plants yet were not. They lacked bones or eyes and sat motionless in the sand. There were colorful corals that resembled rocks but were not rocks. There were oysters and barnacles and other animals that had brains and were just as alive as the fish that swam above. The biologist had collected them all from the shallows near the island.

"Genus *Clav-e-lina*," Luke said, touching a finger to the glass.

It was the Latin name for a rubbery-looking glob known as a sea squirt, or tunicate. The purple glob lay on the bottom of a tank. Knowing the Latin names of various creatures, the biologist had said, was important. It avoided the confusion of "local names." The same animal or plant might be known by dozens of different local names, which varied from country to country and language to language. But an animal or plant's Latin, or scientific, name remained the same worldwide.

"Sea squirts don't look like they can swim, but they can," Luke recited. "I'm not sure how. When they're really tiny, I guess. Anyway, at a certain age, sea squirts latch on to a solid object and stay there. They filter dirty water and make it clean. The same with scallop shells, sponges, and oysters. All kinds of plain-looking little animals that filter water. The ocean would be a dirty mess without them."

Dr. Ford, sitting at a desk computer, said, "Good job. Impressive." He was content to listen, not ask questions. There were people, children and adults, as the biologist knew, who did well in life but not on tests.

Nearby, in a portable crib, baby Izaak slept and dreamed, unconcerned.

Luke named several more creatures by their Latin names. Sometimes he had memorized them with a single glance at a book. More often he'd had to write the name over and over before it was anchored in his brain.

Something he had yet to master was how to pronounce complicated words.

"Sea a-nem-o-nees," he struggled to say. "Anemones resemble a stalk of flowers, but they're not plants. They're animals. The difference, I guess, is that plants live off air and sunlight. Animals—no matter what they look like— feed on plants and other animals. How am I doing?"

A week ago, Dr. Ford had suggested the boy learn all he could about taking care of the lab.

"I travel a lot," the biologist had explained, which was

true. The man owned a large, fast boat and a seaplane that could take off or land on water. "It would be nice to leave someone in charge who has an expert knowledge of how things work here. I think you can do it, and I would pay double."

Luke, who had never been an "expert" at anything, was not used to compliments. But he did understand the importance of earning his own keep.

You'll never owe anyone anything but kindness, his mother had said before she died.

"Sure, I could use the money," he had told the biologist.

Now, a week later, here they were, back in the lab, having what seemed to be a friendly talk. But it was obvious that Dr. Ford had something serious on his mind.

The boy feared that he'd screwed up somehow. "There's something I should've told you, I guess," he stammered. "Last week I managed to break your shark-tagging pole. The big one, not the little fiberglass tagger. Stepped on it, maybe, I don't know. Sorry. It won't happen again."

"That old broom handle? So what?"

"Well, I can tell you're upset about something. I'm making you a new pole. Or maybe it's because . . . Sir, I know I'm not good at pronouncing big words. Some of this stuff's hard to learn. I'll do better, Dr. Ford. I promise."

The man's attention shifted to the boy.

"First off, call me Doc. Or Marion. And don't be so hard on yourself. People who learn fast don't always understand what they've learned. What makes you think I'm mad? Even when I am mad—it doesn't happen often—but when I am, almost no one can tell." After a pause, he admitted, "But you're right. I'm upset about something. How'd you know?"

The colors in Luke's head had painted the biologist with a reddish glow. He'd come to associate the color with strong emotion.

"Just a guess," the boy lied.

"I doubt that," Dr. Ford said gently. "Look, you don't have to worry about being honest with me. We're friends. Friends need to trust each other. We should be able to say any darn silly thing that comes into our heads without worrying about the results. Think about that, okay?"

"Sure . . . Doc," Luke said, using the name for the first time to see how it felt. It was sort of like calling an adult "Captain," only not quite as cool. The man's first name, though, definitely wouldn't work. To Luke, the name Marion sounded like a girl's name.

Doc got up, checked on the sleeping baby, then went toward the door, carrying his cell phone. "I've got to make a call. Last night the police found a bunch of dead sharks near Woodring's Point. They want my opinion. Depending on how the sharks died, there's a chance you and the sisters might be able to help identify them. I'll explain when I get back—if you're willing to trust me."

Willing to trust . . .

That was something else the boy had never been asked to do.

Luke stepped closer to one of the bubbling aquariums. A secret world existed on the other side of the glass. A few weeks ago, he would have noticed only the slow chaos of swirling fish.

That had changed. Now, in the boy's mind, the rubbery purple globs, the strands of sea grasses, the nuggets of coral all came to life. Each creature had a name. Each was set apart in the boy's head. Yet all were connected to the secret world inside the tank, and the secrets of the bay that lay sparkling and blue through the window.

Soon Luke was lost in the beauty of something that, a few weeks ago, had seemed too complex for a kid like him to understand.

EIGHT
SHARK KILLERS!

The Estéban sisters and Hannah were still outside when the biologist returned from making a phone call. The man checked on the baby again, took his seat at the computer, and tried to pick up the conversation where he and Luke had left off.

He didn't seem to notice that the boy, who'd been staring into an aquarium, was startled as if awakening from a dream.

Or maybe the biologist did.

"Are you okay?" he asked.

"Yeah, sure . . . Doc," Luke said. It felt okay calling the biologist that.

Doc, smiling, seemed to appreciate the effort. "Tell

you what: I'll be honest with you, but it's entirely your call whether to be honest with me. How's that sound? "

"Uh, good, I guess," Luke said. "What do you mean?"

"It means whatever you say is fine. I'm curious about something. I've spent a lot of time on the water. I know you weren't guessing when you saw that bull shark way before the rest of us did. And you weren't guessing when you said the shark would surface beside the boat. It impressed the heck out of me, but your aunt Hannah is worried. She says you've changed since the day you were struck by lightning. Care to talk about it?"

The boy stared at the floor. "I figured she told you about what happened. That's why you hired me, isn't it? 'Cause she thinks I'm screwed up somehow and acting strange. You felt sorry for me."

"I did it as a favor to Hannah, yeah," Doc admitted. "At first, but not now. You've proven yourself, as far as I'm concerned. I mean it. You show up on time and you're a hard worker. So far I've yet to hear you complain about anything, and you don't make excuses—that's a biggie with me. Another biggie is, when something needs to be done, you do it without having to be told. That's rare in kids your age"—the man's face showed amusement—"and just as rare when it comes to a lot of adults. Seriously, I want to keep working with you, Luke. You've been a big help around here."

Luke, who hadn't cried since his mother's funeral, felt dangerously close to tears. He continued to gaze at the floor.

Doc asked, "Do you think you've changed since it happened?"

"The storm? Maybe. I'm lucky to be alive, I guess."

"Very lucky. I did a little research and printed it out." The man opened a drawer. He pushed a manila envelope across the desk. "Getting struck by lightning could've crippled you for life or messed up your brain forever. The results are usually worse than people can imagine. But there are a few exceptions—like you . . . *maybe*."

The boy sensed what the biologist suspected, but said, "I don't get what you mean."

"I think you do. It's rare—one out of a hundred million, maybe. But lightning-strike victims occasionally notice positive changes. Changes that are mysterious in a way that doctors still don't understand."

"Even you?"

The biologist found that funny. "Especially me. There

are case histories in there." He touched the manila envelope. There was a woman—you can read about her yourself—who survived a lightning strike. This woman, she was in her early twenties when it happened. Her whole life, she'd been convinced that she was terrible at mathematics because she'd failed algebra in high school. Then, for reasons no one can explain, she became fascinated by geometry while she was recovering in the hospital. Now she's going to night school, getting her college degree."

"Because she was struck by lightning," Luke said.

The man pressed his lips together—thoughtful or skeptical, the boy couldn't tell—then answered carefully. "The woman probably believes that lightning caused the change. I'm sure there are a lot of people who want to believe it's true. But personally"—he shook his head—"I think it's unlikely. Stick with me here. There's another case history for you to read."

The biologist opened the envelope. "A man in his forties, he'd been playing golf in a thunderstorm—which suggests the guy wasn't too smart to begin with. This guy loved music his entire life, but he'd been told as a kid that he had zero musical talent. I forget the details—they're in there." Again, he indicated the envelope. "Anyway, this guy, who had never played the piano, suddenly began compos-ing music when he got out of the hospital. I printed several other case histories for you. Those are just two examples of normal people who woke up with what some might think are superhuman gifts. There's a term for that sort of abrupt change—savant syndrome."

"Say-vant what?" Luke asked.

The biologist explained. "A savant is a sort of genius at certain things but has no formal training. Ever heard the term before?"

"I'm no genius," the boy said, as if the idea were ridicu-lous. "I'm smart enough to know that."

Doc found that remark funny, too. "*Genius* is just an-other word for *talent*," he replied gently. "Or an unusual gift. Everyone has a genius of some type. I'm not trying to be nice. There're studies that prove it. Most people have talents they don't know they have for one reason or an-other. A lack of confidence, usually. Laziness, sometimes. Or fear."

"Fear?"

"Oh yeah. There are all kinds of fear—fear of failure. Fear of the hard work it takes to accomplish something great. Fear of not being smart enough or not being good enough." In a wry tone, the biologist added, "Our brains are brilliant when it comes to inventing reasons to be afraid. It's even better at avoiding anything that seems difficult."

"I used to be scared of a lot of things," Luke admitted. "I don't know why, but now I don't feel so scared—except maybe what'll happen if I change back to normal."

"Ah, back to normal, huh?" Doc said. "I thought so. So you really are convinced that getting struck by lightning has changed you for the better."

Luke was unsure. "Maybe. Do you think the changes will go away?"

Doc waited until the boy looked up from the floor. "Lightning isn't magic, Luke. Electricity can't give you something you didn't have to begin with. The woman who suddenly liked geometry—she probably had a talent for math before she was struck. Just didn't realize because she'd never really tried. The same with the guy who's now composing music on a piano. That's what *I* think. It's possible they'd been told so often they didn't have any talent, they ignored their own gifts. That might be true of you."

Luke sensed he was being lectured. That was typical of adults, but it somehow seemed different coming from the biologist, who seldom spoke unless there was a good reason. The boy was starting to feel comfortable talking, just the two of them, him and Doc, alone in a laboratory with only fish around to hear.

"I don't care anything about being special," Luke said. "I hate the idea of people thinking I'm, you know, weird or something. And they will—kids at school, especially—if they see the burn scars on my"—he motioned with his hand—"and on my shoulder. I hope those *do* go away. I suppose my aunt told you about the scars, too."

"They're called fractal patterns," Doc said.

"Frack—you mean like freckle patterns?" the boy asked.

"Fractal, as in fragments. They're partial patterns found in nature. I did a little research on those, too." He reached into the envelope and spread out several photographs. "Have a look—pictures of people who've been struck by lightning and survived. You have to admit they're not typical scars." He spread the photos across the desk. "Hannah says the burns on your hand and shoulder are more like tattoos. *Beautiful tattoos*—those were her exact words. Mind if I examine them?"

Luke wasn't wild about the idea. But okay. He pulled off his right glove, opened his hand, and held it up as if stopping traffic. The burn mark on his palm was a complex pattern of swirls, straight lines, and loops.

The biologist adjusted his glasses. "Hmm . . . the scar is fainter than I expected. Is it okay if I—" He reached for a magnifying glass and used it for a closer look. Satisfied, he placed the glass on the desk. "You know what that scar is, don't you? It's a perfect diagram of the nerves under the skin of your hand—probably where the lightning entered or exited." Fascinated, the man nodded. "Remarkable. This is absolutely exact in every detail. Is the one on your shoulder similar?"

The boy pulled his sleeve up.

"Interesting . . . yeah. Extraordinary, even. Hannah was right." The man sat back, impressed. "Your so-called scars are better than any tattoos I've ever seen. Know why? Because they're real. They're part of who you are—not something dreamed up by some guy in a tattoo shop. And certainly nothing to be ashamed of. Luke, I wouldn't try to hide what happened to you from Maribel and Sabina. They're already curious, and they're smart. They'll figure it out."

"It's none of their business," Luke said, and pulled his sleeve down.

"It is now," Doc replied. He was smiling. "You're working

together, and they're curious about . . . well, think about it. This is Florida. You can't wear gloves all the time."

The boy didn't like being the center of attention, so he said he'd think about it. It took a while to shift the subject to the dead sharks the biologist had mentioned.

"That's what I was upset about," Doc said. "I was reading an e-mail from a friend who's a fish and wildlife officer. Around here they used to be called the marine patrol—like police officers. That's who I went outside to call. Here, I'll show you."

He turned the computer screen for the boy to see. "Yesterday fifty-three sharks washed ashore on Woodring's Point—that's only a few miles from here. A dozen of them were still alive. The rest were dead. I get alerts about criminal activity if it concerns anything that swims or lives in the ocean. "

"Blacktip sharks?" Luke asked.

"They haven't been positively identified," the biologist said. "The police knew the twelve sharks that were still alive couldn't be saved. So they put them on ice for me to examine. They needed an expert opinion because the fins on all fifty-three sharks had been cut off. You know what that means when it comes to positively identifying a shark."

Yes, the boy knew. Many sharks were nearly identical in appearance except for the color and shape of their fins.

Luke said, "Then it was done on purpose, you think?" He waited for the man to confirm it was true. "That really sucks. Shark-fin soup, just like you told us. Do you think someone cut them off to sell? No one could like soup enough to slaughter fifty-some sharks just for their fins."

The biologist got up, messed with baby Izaak's blankets for a while, and walked to a window with a view of the bay. "Maybe bait fishermen killed them. But more likely those sharks were caught in a net," he said. "All fifty-three were caught in the same spot, or they wouldn't have washed ashore together. Whoever did it knew they were breaking the law. So they were in a hurry. They cut the fins off while the sharks were still alive and dumped them. I don't know how a dozen of those fish managed to stay alive until they washed ashore."

"Cut their fins off while they were still—" The boy couldn't finish the sentence. "That's about the sickest thing I've ever heard of."

Doc responded, "Well, it's cruel, at the very least. A shark without fins can't breathe for very long. It's not a good way to die. I think someone is targeting the summer blacktip migration. If the poachers are still in the area, it's likely they fish at night and hide out during the day. That's what the police think, anyway. So far they don't have a clue who's doing it."

Luke knew what *poachers* meant. In Ohio, they were hunters who trespassed and killed animals for sport or profit, not food. Like the biologist, Luke was slow to anger, but he felt his jaw clench. "Greedy criminals are what those creeps are. I hope the police put them in jail."

"Or they're people desperate for money," Doc reasoned. "Either way, you're right. What they did was cruel—and illegal. They know it, and they don't want to get caught. That makes them dangerous. Keep that in mind if you happen to see net fishermen when you and the girls are out in a boat. Very few netters are criminals. Even so, it would be best to avoid them."

"But you'd be there with us, right?" Luke replied. "Or Hannah?"

Doc thought for a moment, then spoke as if Luke was a trusted friend. "This is between you and me, okay? Hannah wanted to surprise you, but I'm going to tell you now. She's turning you and the sisters loose to fish on your own tomorrow morning. Just you three as a team."

"Really?"

"You've earned it," Doc said. "Maribel will be named captain—let's face it, that girl's better than most adults when it comes to running a boat. But I'm appointing you to special lookout duty. Do you know what that means?"

Luke was eager to please this nice, easygoing man with thick wire-rimmed glasses. "Yeah, sure. Keep my eyes and ears open, and . . . what else? Stay away from the shark poachers if we see them, I guess."

"No one is better qualified to see what most people can't see," the man replied wryly. Then he became serious. "Luke, uh . . . I want to ask you something else. You have really good eyesight. I mean, truly unusual. Have you ever had your eyes tested?"

"Like, test me to see if I need glasses?" Luke thought back to the fifth grade at the little farm school he had attended. "They brought in a nurse who took us into a room where there was an eye chart on the wall. I guess I did okay. Some of the kids had to get glasses. I didn't."

The man wanted to know more. "Did the nurse say your eyesight is twenty-twenty? That's normal for most people. From twenty feet away, the letters on an eye chart appear the same to the average person. See how it works? Twenty-twenty. That's normal eyesight."

Unsure, the boy shook his head.

"A person with poor vision, someone like me," Doc explained, "might score twenty-thirty. Or twenty-forty. Take off my glasses, I can only see letters that an average person can see from thirty or forty feet away. But someone with really good eyesight might score twenty-fifteen."

Luke was starting to get it. "The lower the second number, the better their eyesight."

"Exactly. Twenty-fifteen, for instance. What that means is they can see letters from twenty feet that an average person can only see from fifteen feet away. Back in Ohio, after you read the eye chart, do you remember the nurse assigning you a score?"

The boy had to search his memory. There were still some blank areas after being struck by lightning. "Maybe," he said. "I remember this guy, this nurse, saying something, but it wasn't two numbers. It was only one number."

"Only one?" Doc was puzzled. "That can't be right."

"I'm pretty sure. The number the guy said was . . . twenty-eight, I think."

The biologist cleared his throat. He found a pencil

and wrote *28* on a notepad. "Is this what you heard the nurse say?"

"Just one number. Yeah."

"Remarkable," the man murmured. Then, in a normal voice, he said, "I think what the nurse told you is this." He crossed out *28* and made one number into two numbers by writing *20/8*. "Understand now?"

The boy stared at the paper. "It means I've got pretty good eyes, I guess."

"Good?" Doc said, snorting the way people do when impressed. "Pal, you are one very unusual young man if I'm right about this. Eagles, certain predatory fish—like sharks, for instance— Well, researchers have set up tests, and a shark's eyesight is only slightly better than yours if that's what the nurse—"

Wild yelps of laughter from outside interrupted what the biologist was about to say. Luke was relieved. He got up and hurried to the screen door to see what all the commotion was about.

Doc remained at his desk. "Hannah's got another surprise for you kids. Go on out and have a look. We'll talk more later." Then he stared at the paper where he'd scribbled *20/8* and muttered, "Truly remarkable."

Luke was already out the door. He trotted down the steps to Maribel and Sabina. They wore brand-new navy-blue T-shirts and long-billed fishing caps. When he saw the bright gold letters on the fronts of the shirts, he grinned. "Sharks Incorporated. That's pretty cool."

The biologist had come out to the upper deck to watch. "Thanks, Doc," Luke called to him. "You don't have to worry about us. I'll keep my eyes open."

NINE
A FUNERAL OR A PARTY?

Maribel was very nervous. Aside from a part-time job babysitting—usually for Izaak—she'd never been in charge of anyone but herself. Now she had been appointed as the captain of a boat.

Hannah noticed Maribel's unease and walked with her along the path toward the marina. "Are you worried about tomorrow?" she asked. "I was so nervous the night before my first fishing charter, I couldn't sleep."

"A little," Maribel admitted. "Mostly about Sabina. What if I give an order and my sister just laughs at me? Or Luke, although I've yet to hear him laugh. It would ruin everything if I had to bring one of them back to the marina."

"Easy answer," the woman replied. "Good captains

don't give orders—unless it's an emergency. They ask their crew for help. Being in charge of a boat isn't nearly as easy as most people think. It means you have to do all the boring, dirty little jobs that no one else wants. It means taking care of your passengers first and yourself last. Do that, and Sabina will *want* to help you."

Maribel wasn't so sure.

An official-looking truck with police lights was parked outside the marina store. Two officers in uniforms hefted a heavy box off the tailgate. They carried the box toward the docks, where boats floated in a listless row of watery blue and pelicans dozed in the heat.

"What's going on?" the girl wondered.

"If it's what I think, you won't like it," Hannah responded. "Last night someone killed a bunch of sharks for their fins. The police brought a few here for Doc to examine."

Maribel was glad that it was Luke standing next to the cleaning table while the biologist cut open the first of a dozen sharks. The man had already identified them all as blacktips for the police.

In Cuba, Maribel had done her share of cutting and cleaning, too. Every Sunday her job was to choose one of the family chickens to kill for dinner. Or fillet a fish she'd bought for a few pesos at the wharf. She didn't enjoy the chore, yet it was necessary.

Not until she visited a Florida supermarket had the girl seen rows of fish and meat neatly wrapped in plastic. It was as if the fare had come from a vending machine, not an animal that had lived and breathed a few days earlier.

Maribel was sensitive. People probably found it easier to eat what they had not seen die. Her, too. She preferred not to eat meat or fish, but sometimes there was no choice—like in Cuba after the hurricane. Or after the lightning storm that had burned down their house. Both she and Sabina knew what it was like to go to bed hungry.

Even so, the sight of small sharks lying on ice, some with their bellies slit open, made the girl wince. These beautiful fish had been discarded like trash by the criminals who had caught them. The sharks were all scarred with ragged craters where their fins and tails had once been.

The police were gone. A group of tourists had gathered on the dock to watch the biologist do a postmortem on the blacktips. Overhead, seagulls battled to grab whatever fell into the water below.

Sabina pushed her way to Maribel's side. The girl took one look at the dead sharks and sputtered three harsh words in Spanish.

"No swearing," Maribel warned. "*Mamá* wouldn't like it. Listen to what Dr. Ford has to say. We might learn something."

The biologist wore an apron and long rubber gloves. Within easy reach were two sharp knives and a water hose on a rough wooden table. One by one, he opened the sharks, removed the organs, and explained to observers what they were seeing.

Most fish had swim bladders that kept them afloat. "A sack of air," the biologist said, that allowed the fish to hang motionless in the water. Sharks did not have swim bladders. The instant they were born they had to swim, or they would sink to the bottom.

"For some sharks, living on the bottom is okay," Doc explained. "They prefer hiding in caves, between rocks sometimes, waiting for food to pass by. It's a myth that all sharks die if they stop swimming. Nurse sharks and a few other species do just fine if they settle where water filters through their gills. But even they would drown without fins."

He flipped a shark over, saying it was easy to tell the difference between male and female sharks. With a knife, he indicated a pair of long, bony-looking spines, or claspers, near the pelvic fin. "This one's a male," he said. "Females don't have claspers. Let's see what's inside his belly."

Doc used the knife, opened the belly, and spoke to Luke. "See? No air sack. Instead, to help with buoyancy, sharks have this huge liver." Two long, dark, fleshy segments were pulled aside. "What we won't find in here is something that people and most fish have—a bladder for processing urine. Sharks expel liquid waste through their skin."

The absence of a bladder, he said, could give the flesh an ammonia taste if it wasn't handled properly.

Luke spoke loud enough for the sisters to hear. "Sharks are good to eat?"

Doc replied, "I think so. Especially cooked over a fire. Take a whiff of the belly and tell me what you think." He stepped aside so the boy could use his nose. "These fish were iced right away, so they're fresh."

That's when the biologist noticed Maribel and Sabina trying to see through the crowd of adults.

"Folks," he announced, "do you mind letting my assistants through? They've been tagging sharks for almost two weeks. This is their first chance to see what's inside the fish they've been catching."

Surprisingly, as the crowd parted, some of the onlookers applauded. Sabina, wearing her new T-shirt, beamed and marched straight to the cleaning table. Maribel lagged behind, saying, "Excuse us . . . sorry," to adults who let them pass. Even Luke was pleased by the attention they were receiving, yet was reluctant to show it.

"Sharks are okay to eat—if you like fish," the boy informed the sisters, as if he were suddenly an expert.

"It can depend on what they've been eating," Doc said. "One more to go, so let's see what's inside."

He placed the last shark on the table and used the smallest knife to open its stomach and intestines. The stomach was huge, even bigger than the animal's liver. Inside the stomach were the remains of several creatures. There was a freshly swallowed fish . . . a large, glove-shaped claw off a crab . . . and then a long, sharp spine of some type was removed.

The biologist held the spine up in the afternoon sunlight. The spine was ivory-white, with a needlelike tip, and jagged on both sides.

"This shark ate a little stingray before he died," the man said. He handed the spine to Luke—who was wearing gloves, of course—and spoke to the sisters. "We found stingray spines in most of these blacktips, didn't we, Luke? Pass it around. It'll help you understand why you've got to be careful if you catch a stingray. Catfish spines are similar. And just as painful if one sticks you. They're venomous—remember that."

Maribel watched the biologist return the shark to the box where eleven others were covered with ice.

"What happens to them now?" she asked.

Doc sighed. "I don't know. I hate to waste them. You'll need chum if you're going to fish in the morning, I guess. You could grind them up. Otherwise, I'll ask around. If someone doesn't want shark steaks for dinner"—he glanced at the crowd of people—"I guess I'll have to cart these back to where they came from."

Sabina didn't like the sound of that. "Dump them like garbage? You can't. We'd be no better than the thieves who killed them. What we should do is have a funeral and bury them. Something nice with candles. I know how—I've buried three cats."

She noticed the odd expression on Luke's face, and stepped back in disgust. "Don't look at me that like that, farm boy. Of course my cats were dead when I buried them. What kind of person do you think I am?"

Maribel walked away. She couldn't stand the idea of the sharks being killed only for their fins. A funeral for fish that were fresh and good to eat didn't seem right, either.

Sabina tagged along after her. "Now what's the problem? I didn't use any swear words—not in English, I'm pretty sure."

The older girl looked toward the bay. Along the deep-water dock was a row of large boats, most of them expensive. At the far end was their small houseboat. On the roof were potted vegetables and herbs growing in the sunlight. The houseboat had been a shabby wreck until they'd fixed it up and painted and hung nice curtains.

Raising fresh herbs, onions, and chili peppers on the boat had been Maribel's idea. The plants reminded the girl that their mother was working, and fixing dinner was up to her. She did an about-face. Sabina did, too.

The biologist was washing off the table when the sisters returned.

"Leave the sharks with me," Maribel said. "I've cleaned fish before. And I know how to cook. People at the marina might enjoy fish steaks done Cuban-style. And there's enough for everyone."

"Our first party," Sabina announced. This was said in a voice loud enough for all to hear. "I'll make the rice—my sister always overcooks it."

Later, Luke told the sisters that he had plucked chickens and cleaned pheasants and rabbits for dinner, but he didn't eat fish and didn't much care for rice. A tuna sandwich was okay, he said, if all the bologna was gone. Or if the house was out of ham. He also liked salami and goose liver.

"Goose what?" The thought made Maribel grimace.

"With lots of mayo," the boy told her. "Sliced pickles, too, if there's not an onion around. Bologna is good fried in a pan with bacon grease. The same with cow tongue, but it's gotta be cut thin. I raised a couple of Angus for 4-H."

"Who is Angus and this 4-H person?" Sabina wanted to know.

"It's not a person. 4-H is a club for farm kids," he replied.

"Two members of the club were named Angus? That's strange," the girl remarked. "They must have been related. What happened to the Angus brothers? Or were they sisters?"

"For cripes' sake, they weren't 4-H members," Luke said. "An Angus is . . . well, the way I raised them, anyway, they're grain-fed heads of beef. When they were fat enough, I sold them at auction at the county fair. On the hoof, of course. I'm not a butcher."

Sabina stared at the strange boy who always wore gloves. "Where is this town called Ohio?" she asked. "People there must live like savages. I bet it takes them five months in Miami to live in Florida legally. It only took us *two*."

Luke was good at ignoring kids of all ages. The same with adults.

They stood near the docks in an area shaded by palms on which coconuts grew in high, heavy clusters among dark-green fronds. Nearby was a barbecue pit made of bricks, where they'd built a fire. A bed of glowing coals drizzled wood smoke up through a web of iron grating. Laid out on a picnic table was food Maribel had chosen to prepare.

She had cleaned and skinned the shark steaks. The slabs of fish were soaking in bowls of spices, ice, and milk. Potatoes were buried among the hot coals. This was Luke's idea. He'd done a lot of camping in Ohio, sometimes alone. Several pineapples, a stalk of bananas, small yellow limes, and some other fruit—all picked by hand—awaited Maribel's attention.

It had taken the trio two hours to get ready for the party. And there was still a lot to do.

That's what Maribel's offer to make dinner for a dozen people had become—a party. CDs from Havana provided music. Conga drums and guitars thrummed from nearby speakers. Adults congregated on the docks and let the three "shark taggers" do what, Maribel insisted, didn't require outside help.

"It'll be good practice for tomorrow," she had confided to Captain Hannah.

After all, if she couldn't organize making dinner, what hope was there for her as the captain of a boat?

Sabina and Luke had helped without complaint. Readying the food had led to a discussion of what they liked to eat. Then to recipes, when Luke claimed he had learned to cook at an early age.

"What kind of parent teaches children to eat tongue from a cow?" Sabina wondered.

"Mom and I would build a fire," the boy replied, "and roast it on a stick. She said buffalo tongue is better. Never tried it, but I would. I wonder if they raise buffalo here in Florida?"

"Animal tongue . . . on *a stick*." Sabina made a face, then addressed her sister. "I've always wanted to go to California where they make movies. Would we have to go through Ohio to get there? I hope not. Ohio must be a terrible place."

"I need three big banana leaves for cooking," Maribel replied. It was best, she had learned, to request help rather than to give an order. "The leaves have to be cut and washed. No soap, though, just fresh water."

"Banana leaves for cooking?" Luke said this in a way that meant *You've got to be kidding*. "Where are we gonna find banana trees?" he asked. Then answered his own question by remembering who had brought the stalk of bananas that lay on the picnic table.

It was a man named Tomlinson. Tomlinson was a kindly but sort of strange, scarecrow-looking guy who lived alone on a sailboat. He was close friends with Doc and Hannah and everyone who lived or worked at the marina.

"Make it five banana leaves," Maribel decided. "The biggest, greenest leaves you can find. Two for cooking, and one leaf for every table. We'll serve food on them—Cuban-style."

The boy hailed Pete, the dog, with a wave of his hand. Sabina trotted after them to the boat ramp. Tomlinson, his long hair in dreadlocks, sat there cross-legged on an upside-down canoe. The man had an easygoing, fun way of speaking. And he dressed like no one Luke had ever seen in Ohio.

"Banana trees, sure," Tomlinson said. "I like the way you kids roll."

The man got up and straightened the scarlet sarong he wore knotted around his waist. His shirt was a faded tank top that showed his skinny ribs. "Fab idea, using banana leaves. They're better than paper plates and make it easier to eat with your hands."

Tomlinson led them toward a mound of brilliant

green leaves visible above the fence beyond the mechanic's shed.

"They're not really trees," he informed Luke and Sabina. "Bananas are plants. Actually, a sort of flowering herb that grows in patches. Tall as trees, sure, but, you know, like a whole different deal. I get psyched just seeing them. Bananas, the ones that grow wild here on the island, are a jillion times sweeter than bananas you buy in stores. Don't you think?"

Sabina agreed and chattered back and forth with the man as they walked. In the shed was a long knife that the girl recognized as a machete. Tomlinson used it to hack off half a dozen giant leaves. They were long, glossy, and shaped like canoes. She and Luke hefted the leaves over their shoulders and carried them toward the picnic area, where they could see Maribel working away.

"That guy's nice but kinda strange," Luke remarked. "Never seen a man wear a red dress before."

Sabina retorted, "He's probably never seen a boy who wears gloves all the time, either."

A while later, she added, "Besides, it's not a dress. It's a sarong. I love sarongs. When I have enough money, the first thing I'll buy—after an iPhone, of course—will probably be a beautiful silk sarong." Then she spoke in a shy tone the boy had never heard her use before. "Do you think I'd look okay in a sarong? I'm not tall like Maribel. But I *will* be one day. What color should I choose?"

Luke hated questions like that. "I'm starving," he said. "I still don't understand why your sister needs banana leaves for cooking."

When dinner was ready, though, Luke realized he'd been wrong about the large green leaves. They made perfect platters for exotic fruits he'd never tried. Chilled mangoes were as sweet as peaches, only better. Bowls of black bean soup were similar to pinto beans cooked with ham. Sabina suggested he drizzle lime juice over the soup and add a sprinkle of fresh chili peppers.

The combination made the boy's eyes water. The girl was surprised—and a tad disappointed—when he asked for more hot chili peppers.

It was Luke's turn to be surprised when he'd finished waiting tables, and went through the line with a plate. The shark steaks were flaky white, thatched with sear marks, and hot from the grill. The steaks were served with butter, wedges of lime, and a tart salsa of tomatoes, onions, and avocado. He had never seen this pearlike fruit with a soft, nutty flavor.

"Ah-vo-cah-dough," the name of the fruit was pronounced.

When Luke took his first bite of shark steak, Sabina knew what he was going to say, which was "Holy moly . . . this is a lot better than tuna fish."

Two bites later, the strange boy announced, "Yeah, really good. Maybe even better than fried bologna."

TEN
FISH THAT OINK, AND A WARNING

After two trips without catching a shark, Maribel began to wonder if she was bad luck. Maybe she was. If she could have predicted what would happen on this day, their third trip alone without an adult, she would not have gotten in the boat and left the dock.

The trio had fished on Tuesday and Wednesday without a problem. There had been no accidents or arguments, yet all they'd caught were catfish. Lots of them. Saltwater catfish, unlike the freshwater variety, weren't good to eat, they had been told. Worse, saltwater catfish were slimy creatures that oinked like pigs until they had been freed by a tool called a hook remover.

"Nothing like pigs," Luke had disagreed. "Pigs are clean, not covered with a bunch of greasy gunk. And they're smarter than horses, my grandpa says."

He'd been freeing a catfish at the time.

"Disgusting," Sabina had agreed. "Let's fish somewhere else. Why do we always have to anchor in the same place every day?"

By the end of their second trip, Maribel had heard that complaint too many times to count. Catching sharks had seemed easy with Captain Hannah or the biologist aboard. Suddenly it was not.

Today would be different, the young captain had told herself when she awoke that morning.

She was right.

What happened on this Thursday morning was different—and much, much worse.

Luke was up early on Thursday and caught a ride with Captain Hannah and the baby to the marina. Doc waved to them from the upper deck of the lab. His pretty blue-and-white seaplane, the boy noticed, was moored close to shore. This was unusual.

Luke also noticed Maribel sitting alone, already rigging their tackle, where the rental boats were moored. She appeared so glum that an ashy-gray color floated into the boy's head. He was learning to associate a person's mood with various colors. What he saw in his head wasn't always accurate, but sometimes it was. The color, ash gray, suggested that the girl was worried about something. He guessed it was because they had yet to catch a shark without an adult along.

That was a disappointment for more than one reason. There had been no excuse to show the sisters the shark-tagging pole he had made. Luke thought his creation was pretty darn impressive. Instead of a broom handle, he had used a splintered limb from the tree that had been struck by lightning. It had taken hours of work. Lots of sanding, then several coats of polish to make the wood shine. His grandfather's drill and some glue had been required to secure the steel dart at the end of the pole.

Until they caught a shark, though, the tagging pole would remain hidden in the boat as a surprise.

Otherwise, it was a slow, sleepy morning on the bay. Mist drifted off the water. Pelicans hung heavily in branches while mullet leaped and smacked the surface for no reason—none that made sense to a boy from Ohio, anyway.

The curly-haired retriever, Pete, appeared. He came charging at Luke full speed, tail wagging. Luke scratched the dog's belly, then focused on a bucket of fish scraps left last night outside the office door.

The retriever's ears perked up with interest.

In his mind, the boy pictured the word *Fetch* and nodded for emphasis.

The dog bolted away. Pete found the bucket's handle, and returned at a trot carrying ten pounds of fish scraps.

Good dog, Luke thought. After playing for a while, he added, *Don't bother me while I'm working.*

The retriever complied by collapsing in the shade and falling asleep.

Every day this week it had been the same. Luke would motion and give a silent command, and the dog obeyed. Usually a training session followed that included fetching balls from the water. As a baseball player, Luke had a pretty good arm. He could throw a ball a long way. To improve his abilities as a fisherman and to provide a greater challenge for the dog, he had begun tying a stick to the line of a fishing rod. After some practice, he could cast the stick twice as far as he could throw it. And with almost the same accuracy.

The dog was an incredible swimmer—could even dive underwater and retrieve objects from the bottom.

But there was no time for play this morning. The boy had to get ready to tag sharks.

All members of Sharks Incorporated had jobs to do before a trip. Maribel was in charge of the boat and fishing tackle. Sabina was responsible for providing a sack lunch, packing a first-aid kit, and making sure they had plenty of water.

Luke's job was making chum. It was a stinky job, but he didn't mind.

He placed a second bucket near his feet and clamped an old metal meat grinder to the side of the cleaning table. The wooden handle reminded him of sausage grinders he'd seen at farm auctions. Luke had never made sausage. Maybe he would one day. It couldn't be any harder than grinding up skins and skeletons of fish that had been filleted and left behind by yesterday's fishermen.

The process was simple: load fish scraps into the top of the grinder and crank hard. Metal blades inside churned it all into a chunky paste that dropped into the bucket below. Later, when the mess was hung in a bag off the boat, tiny pieces would drift away in an oily sheen. Fish from a long, long way off would smell the chum and come searching for the source.

Today, hopefully, those fish would include blacktip sharks.

Luke didn't mind hard, smelly work. It gave his mind time to roam. Daydreams, images of him in a Major League Baseball uniform were standard. Lately, though, he'd been trying hard to *think*, not just daydream.

Trying to understand the colors that sometimes flashed in his head gave him something to do. Like now. What he thought of as his "lightning eye" moved to Maribel. The girl *was* unhappy about something. No . . . he'd been right the first time. She was worried about today's trip. The ashen-gray haze still framed her face.

Luke's focus moved to Sabina. The girl had just exited the houseboat where her family lived. Black braids dangled from beneath her new fishing cap. She wore sneakers, baggy shorts, and her blue Sharks Incorporated T-shirt. The girl appeared happy, yet in his mind an orange-yellow strobe trailed the girl as she came toward him.

The orange-yellow light throbbed in a way that reminded Luke of something. Finally it came to him: a caution light at a dangerous intersection. That was strange. He'd never experienced flashing orange colors before.

"*Buenos días*," the girl said.

Good morning? Suddenly, Luke wasn't so sure it would be a good morning. He associated Sabina with a soft blue mist. And sometimes yellow sparks that turned red when she was mad. Which was often. But why a flashing orange caution light?

"Hope so," he mumbled.

"What's that supposed to mean?" Sabina placed the sack she was carrying, which contained the day's lunch, on the dock. After wondering if the food was too close to the chum bucket, she moved the sack to a place where the air was fresher.

"I made a bologna sandwich just for you," she informed the boy. "Talk about gross. And sliced mangoes with black beans and salsa. If I'd known you were grumpy, I wouldn't have bothered."

Luke shrugged and reached for more fish scraps.

With an expression of distaste, the girl watched him crank the handle. "Maybe you're doing it wrong," she said. "Maybe that's why we haven't caught any sharks. Let me borrow your gloves—I'll show you the right way."

Luke's inner eye moved from Sabina to her older sister. The caution light flashed brighter in his mind.

Then, for reasons he didn't understand, a distant area of the bay attracted his attention. It was a narrow opening in the mangroves where the trees were taller. Fishing guides called the spot Fools Cut. He'd been told it was because there were rocky oyster bars that made it dangerous to pass through. Oyster shells were rock-hard, sharp as razors.

For this reason, few boat captains risked an attempt.

"What's the matter with you?" the girl demanded. She was irritated by the boy's distracted, faraway gaze. "You think I enjoy slicing bologna for someone who won't even talk about sarongs . . . or loan me a pair of dirty gloves?"

Luke seemed to notice her for the first time. "Sorry . . . I've got a funny feeling about today," he said.

Anyone but Sabina would've been startled by this odd response.

"I *know*," she said in a superior way. "It's because you're strange . . . even stranger than me. Why are you ashamed of your hand?"

The boy stopped cranking. "I'm not ashamed," he said, and stared for moment. "Who told you about my hand?"

The girl was delighted. "You told me, farm boy, without saying a word. Sometimes I know what's in your head. Like just now, you were thinking there's a better place to catch sharks. Same with me. The difference is, I'm not afraid to tell my snotty sister."

That wasn't what Luke had been thinking.

A little later, lugging the chum bucket toward the boat, he didn't respond when the girl suggested, "Take off your gloves, and I'll read your fortune. Don't worry. I won't tell anyone what I see."

Luke wondered, *How dumb does she think I am?*

The rental boat was an open and simple craft. It was similar to a fiberglass sled with bench seats. In the middle of the boat was a steering wheel on the console. Along the sides were storage hatches where the new tagging pole was hidden. Maribel stood at the wheel and steered toward the mouth of the bay. She couldn't help noticing that something had changed between her sister and Luke. Usually, the pair chose seats as far apart as possible.

Not this trip.

They sat side by side, close enough that Sabina could jabber away without being heard over the noise of the engine. Mostly the boy ignored her. But sometimes he seemed interested in what she had to say.

That, too, was odd.

Maribel concentrated on staying in the channel.

The boat wasn't fast, but traveling twenty miles an hour across the water felt fast. Wind tangled her hair. Seagulls scouted their wake, hoping to snare small fish the boat had spooked. The roaring engine vibrated the deck beneath her feet. The air smelled wonderful—a mix of salt, wet sand, and mangrove swamp.

Driving required concentration. It also gave Maribel time to plan today's fishing trip.

Last night, she had sought advice from Captain Hannah. Who better to ask? The woman had been on the covers of fishing magazines and had appeared on TV shows.

"I have to be doing something wrong," Maribel had

confided. "Sabina's already complaining. And I think Luke is losing confidence in me. I've been anchoring in exactly the same spot where we caught sharks with you and Dr. Ford. But, two trips in a row, all we caught were catfish."

Hannah had spent a patient hour with the girl, offering tips and studying a map of the bay. Nautical maps were called charts, as Maribel knew.

"You don't catch fish just by baiting a hook," Hannah had said. "The most important tools are your eyes and your brain. First, figure out where the fish *should* be. That can take some time. Think of it this way: When people are hungry, where do they go?"

"The kitchen?" Maribel had guessed.

"Where there's plenty of food," the woman had agreed. "Sharks are no different. On the water, what we might consider to be the kitchen moves around. Sometimes it moves several times a day. Out there"—Hannah had motioned to the water—"tell me this. What else eats fish besides other fish?"

Birds.

"Think of seagulls and pelicans as your scouts," Hannah had said. "They follow schools of baitfish. If you find a school of bait, chances are good there are bigger fish nearby."

Maribel had made mental notes. There were many ways to locate fish before bothering to anchor.

Large fish are predators, according to Hannah. They stalk areas where the current is strong enough to flush smaller fish and crabs out of hiding. Predators use tree roots and rocks as hiding places. They wait for food to swim by.

There is something else that good captains look for, she added. When big fish ambush a school of bait, the feeding frenzy often creates an oily sheen on the water.

"A natural chum slick," the woman said. "Look for it and consider anchoring down current. Let the fish come to you."

"Avoid areas where there's a lot of boat traffic" was another tip Hannah provided. "In shallow water, the fewer boats the better. Maybe you've been anchoring too close to the channel."

The fishing guide had offered lots of good advice.

Maribel was determined to put the advice to use. At the mouth of the bay, she pulled back on the throttle.

As the engine slowed, the young captain remembered that outboard motors leave frothy tracks. She saw that a couple of boats had passed through the area recently. Several more would soon follow.

That wasn't surprising. There was only one marked channel in and out of Dinkins Bay.

"We've decided we don't want to anchor in the same place," Sabina called over the noise. "We want to catch something besides stupid catfish."

Maribel expected this. But good captains give their crew credit for decisions that have already been made, as Hannah had told her. "Great idea," Maribel replied. "I think you're right. We'll look for a better spot."

The expression on Sabina's face told Luke, *See? I told you my sister would listen to me.*

The boy shrugged. He seemed to be fixated on a tiny opening in the distance. Trees were taller there. Fools Cut, the opening was called. The name was also a warning because the cut was guarded by rocks and oyster bars.

Maribel nudged the boat ahead and used her eyes. The tidal current appeared sluggish where they had anchored on previous trips. There were no schools of baitfish that sometimes spattered the surface like rain. No birds, no leaping mullet.

She said, "I think we should move to a whole different area. Anyone have a suggestion?"

In Spanish, Sabina replied, "Let's try outside the bay, where the water is deeper."

Maribel gave the girl a sharp look that meant, *We're not allowed outside the bay, and you know it!*

"Speak English," she added, "so Luke understands."

"When are we going to have Spanish-speaking days?" Sabina complained. "Marion said we would. He said the farm boy needs to learn Spanish because Spanish is just as important as English."

That was true, but now was not the time to discuss it. While the sisters debated the subject Luke continued to stare into the distance.

Maribel liked Luke . . . not in *that* way, of course. Not really. It was because he was quiet and did his work without complaint. He also spooked her a little with his ability to sometimes see what others could not. "Bionic eyes," her sister had termed the gift.

Maybe that gift could help them now.

"What are you looking at?" Maribel asked.

Reluctantly, he replied, "Nothing. Just that little opening in the trees."

"I've never seen a boat anchored there," Maribel replied uneasily. "I heard there's deep water near the mangroves. But it's not easy to get to. That might be good, though. The fewer boats, the more fish. Think we'd find sharks?"

Luke nodded. He *knew* there would be sharks. What else could explain a series of violent explosions on the surface that he could see from half a mile away? He pointed. "Look for yourself. Something big is feeding in that cut."

The girls shaded their eyes. In the distance was an occasional puff of mist that *might* be where a big fish had busted the surface.

"If the farm boy says he sees fish, he sees fish," Sabina said on Luke's behalf.

Maribel was convinced, "Okay, then. Fools Cut. Here we go. We'll take it slow and try to find our way through the oyster bars."

The boy did not mention the orange caution light that once again began to flash softly in his head.

ELEVEN
SMALL SHARKS AND BIG TROUBLE

That Thursday afternoon, they hooked so many sharks and other fish in Fools Cut that Luke forgot he had sensed danger. Or maybe the caution light was a warning about the shoals—areas too shallow for most boats to cross—that guarded the entrance. The colors he saw were often confusing.

Oysters grew on both sides of Fools Cut in clusters beneath the surface—oyster bars, as they're known. They could rip the propeller off a motor. Or slice a person's feet to shreds if someone was foolish enough to get out and walk.

Luke soon learned this the hard way. Maribel had done a good job of snaking their boat through the shoals until the water suddenly went from several feet deep to almost no water at all. When their fiberglass hull crunched against something beneath the surface, she did as they'd been taught. Immediately she shut off the engine and confirmed that the anchor was coiled and ready for use.

"We have to tilt the motor up and use the oars," she said. "No wonder boats don't risk coming through here. We'll have to find another spot."

Luke, who had seen fish exploding on the surface, knew that deep water lay near the mangroves only a few boat lengths away.

"How about if I get out and push?" he suggested, and started untying his shoes. They were red Michael Jordans. He'd purchased the shoes at a yard sale for a tenth of what they'd sold for in a store. They were size eight—a little big for his feet, but so what?

"I don't think that's a good idea," Maribel said. As she spoke, she looked in the direction of Dr. Ford's lab. His house was near the marina, both visible in the distance. Hannah had instructed them not to get out of the boat unless there was an emergency. What if someone saw?

Too late. Luke already had his legs dangling over the side and was adjusting his gloves.

"Wait!" she called. "At least put your shoes on. There could be stingrays."

The memory of the stingray spine Luke had seen was enough to make him comply. He and his red Michael Jordans went over into water that barely covered his ankles. With the engine up, the boat was easy to push despite the rough footing. Oysters crunched like eggshells with every step the boy took. They stabbed at his feet. Soon the water was deep enough, and he vaulted into the boat after a final push.

"Your ankle's bleeding," Sabina scolded, but was actually delighted. "When will you learn to listen to us? Good thing I brought this along."

She couldn't wait to use the first-aid kit. Maribel had already dropped the anchor so the boat wouldn't drift into even more dangerous water.

Luke removed his left shoe and inspected it. The rubber sole looked as if it had been sliced by hundreds of small knives. No cuts on his feet, though. Just a deep slice on his ankle.

"I hope this doesn't sting too much," Sabina said, and sounded as if she meant it. She cleaned the cut with an iodine swab, then added some kind of goop from a tube. Maribel was concerned as well.

The sisters bickered briefly over who would apply Luke's bandage. A bottle of cold water was handed to him. With it came a stern reminder about the importance of drinking lots and lots of water on a hot summer morning.

It had been a long time, the boy realized, since anyone had fussed over him like that.

"Does it hurt?" Maribel asked when they were done.

Hurt? The pain of an oyster cut didn't compare to getting zapped by lightning. Luke was tempted to say this, and possibly even reveal the burn scar on his hand.

Maybe he would one day. The sisters were close to earning his trust. But not now.

Instead, he nodded toward Fools Cut. It was a narrow gap in the mangroves where the current boiled over pools of deep water. The way the water churned reminded him of a river he'd seen in Colorado during a trip with his mother not long before she had died.

Luke shook himself back to the present and searched the surface for fish. *You have to learn to look through the water*, Doc had told them.

There was a trick to it, as the boy was learning. He ignored the water's sunny glare and refocused on what lay beneath the surface. There, drifting in and out of shadows, he saw heavy dark shapes. They were as thick and straight as ax handles. But ax handles could not move with the slow flick of a tail.

These did.

"I have a good feeling about this spot," Luke announced, tying his shoes. "In fact, let's get ready. I want to show you something I made."

He opened a rod locker and, for the first time, revealed the shark-tagging pole. It was a short, lightweight spear with the familiar steel tagging dart for a point. That was the only resemblance to the cracked broom handle he'd broken a week ago. The shaft was amber colored, dense as pine resin. The grain was polished like glass.

"Beautiful," Sabina said. She held out her hands for a closer look. "Where'd you ever get such beautiful wood?"

Luke wasn't ready to discuss the day he, and a tree next to the house, had been struck by lightning. "Found it in the yard," he said in a dismissive way. "Let's hope we get a chance to use it."

At thirteen, Maribel thought herself too old to whoop and laugh like a child. She was the quiet, thoughtful sister. Her clothes were always pressed, her homework done on time, her emotions always, always under control.

But not after three trips as captain without a shark.

When the first blacktip shark hit, Maribel watched in disbelief, then hooted with joy. "Got one!" she hollered. "Luke, grab the rod. Hurry . . . don't let it get away. Sabina—reel in the other line so they don't get tangled."

The younger sister couldn't reel in line—she suddenly had a fish, too. Her rod buckled. The bottle of tea on her lap went flying. Both fishing lines screamed through the narrow swath of water toward blue sky on the other side of the mangroves.

The sharks weren't big. In the bright morning sunlight, they leaped and splashed in the air. They battled until the heavy rods forced them to the boat. Finally, with no adults aboard to help, the trio had the chance to use what they'd learned about shark-tagging protocol.

Maribel had the camera, tags, and data cards ready. With the rod secured, Sabina lifted her shark from the water. Its gray skin was rough like sandpaper. The fins looked metallic black but were a deep dark blue up close. A grapelike membrane over the shark's yellow eyes blinked at the girl while she placed the animal on the gunnel of the boat and used a measuring stick.

"Thirty-four point five inches," she reported.

"Thirty-four point five," Luke echoed to confirm that the measurement was accurate.

Maribel noted the information on a card and snapped photos.

"Weight?"

Sabina used a little hand scale. "Nine . . . almost ten pounds."

"Nine pounds, eight ounces," Luke said looking over her shoulder.

It all went down on the data card.

"How much time do we have?" the younger girl demanded. A shark can't be out of the water for more than three minutes. That was an important part of the shark-tagging protocol they had learned.

"Two minutes, ten seconds" Maribel replied. "You're doing fine."

This was the procedure they had learned. They were getting good at it.

In Sabina's hands, the shark struggled to get away, then went limp when she gently rolled it onto its back.

The biologist had taught them this technique. *Tonic immobility*, he'd termed the behavior. Turn a shark upside down and it would "go to sleep" until returned to the water.

"The anal fin is whitish-gray," Sabina reported. "It's a male. See the claspers?"

"Definitely a male blacktip shark," Luke confirmed after viewing the two spines under its tail. "Not a spinner shark. Ready for the tag?"

The shark was too small to require the new tagging pole. Instead, the boy used a hand dart to insert a tiny plastic capsule behind the dorsal fin.

"Next, the hook remover," he said. He reached for the console where the tools were kept.

When the hook was gone, Sabina cradled the shark and lowered it into the water. The tidal current was strong. She turned the fish's head into the current so that water flowed into its mouth. "How much time?" she asked again.

"I think you broke the speed record," Maribel said. She had the camera to her eye, getting it all on video. "How do the gills look?"

On each side of the shark's head were five flaps, or

vents. The vents moved in a healthy rhythm, pumping water to provide oxygen. "He feels strong as a bull," the girl said. "I'm going to name him El Toro. Make sure to write it on the card."

Sabina had named every shark she'd caught and released.

Luke removed his rod from a rod holder and reeled in the blacktip he had hooked. The fish had been content to cruise along the mangroves close to the boat, but it made a spectacular spinning leap when it felt the pressure of the line.

The procedure was the same, although their duties were reversed. Sabina used the tagging dart. Luke revived and released the fish. Maribel oversaw it all and offered advice when needed.

After watching their second blacktip shark swim away, the boy flashed a rare smile. He said to Maribel, "Good job . . . Captain."

Maribel didn't know how to react. For a sweet few seconds, the voice in her head that criticized and nagged was silenced.

"We're a team," Maribel responded, embarrassed but secretly pleased. "Let's fish a little longer, then have lunch."

Sabina didn't want to stop for lunch, even though she had prepared the food herself. Thanks to good luck—or maybe the farm boy's spooky eyesight—they had anchored in the middle of a school of sharks.

Over the next hour, they landed and tagged thirteen blacktips. This was a new record for an afternoon on the boat. And they'd done it by themselves, no adults along. They had also caught a fish they had never seen, but Luke thought he recognized it from a book.

"A nurse shark," he suggested, but wasn't quite sure. The fish was cinnamon colored. It had a wide mouth and tiny, crushing teeth beneath long, stringy-looking threads of flesh that resembled whiskers.

"I'll leave that part blank until Dr. Ford sees the pictures," Maribel said. She was using a clipboard and a pencil. "Is anyone hungry? We can leave the baits out while we eat."

Sabina was hungry . . . sort of. It was hard to be certain because she had to go to the bathroom. The discomfort had been building all morning. On a day as hot as this, she'd downed several bottles of water and tea from the ice chest, as instructed. Now she needed to go—and she needed to go *soon*.

Luke and Maribel had drunk just as much water. The difference was that they were willing to do what Captain Hannah had suggested when a passenger felt the need to go. They had asked for privacy, turned on music, and carried a bucket to the back of the boat.

Especially Luke. Shy as he was, the boy had requested privacy many more times than Maribel had—every fifteen minutes, it seemed to Sabina, who found this irritating. She had been to parties where less music had been played.

That didn't bother the farm boy one bit, him and his stupid gloves. After an unusually long wait, she had whispered to her sister, "Maybe they kicked him out of Ohio. Those savages probably don't even bother with buckets. I bet they sneak outside like goats."

Maribel had shushed the girl. She had also asked her sister, "Are sure you don't have to . . . you know?"

Use the bucket, Maribel had meant.

Sabina had responded with a hiss, like a cat. "*Never.* I didn't come to all the way from Cuba on a raft to use a bucket."

Now the girl was desperate for relief.

Maribel had opened the lunch sack. Luke was munching a disgusting bologna sandwich. They had repositioned the boat so that it was shaded by mangrove trees. Gnarled limbs hung over the back of the boat in a way that Sabina found tempting. Leaves above her were waxen green. The shoreline was a tangle of roots and shells. But the ground looked solid enough to support a small girl's weight.

Sabina's eyes moved from the bucket to the shoreline. She looked from the shoreline to the bucket, then back to the tangle of roots.

Somewhere in that jungle of green there had to be a private open space.

"Excuse me," Sabina said as if making an announcement. "I've decided to use the . . . *you know*. And don't rush me!"

Immediately, the boy and her sister swiveled to face the front of the boat, although Maribel reminded her, "Make sure to wear your life vest."

Sabina turned the music loud. She waited to confirm no one was looking. When it seemed safe, she reached up, grabbed a tree limb, and shuffled ashore.

I'll be back before they even know I'm gone. That's what Sabina told herself as she disappeared into the bushes.

TWELVE
A GRUESOME DISCOVERY,
A NARROW ESCAPE

Mangrove trees are known as "walking trees." It's because their roots sprout like hoops. The roots thicken and travel. They claim every inch of space until one is tangled into another. When mangroves capture an island, their roots lock together like bars.

The trees actually creep across shallow water to form new islands.

Sabina was beginning to think it was a mistake to sneak away into this forest of shadows and swamp. There were no paths, just one rubbery mangrove root after another. It was impossible to walk in a straight line. For a while, music marked the location of the boat. Soon, though, the girl was confused. The music seemed to change direction with every turn she made.

Sabina was worried that by now Maribel would have noticed she was gone. Her tummy hurt with a building pressure, and a haze of mosquitoes had found her. But she kept going, determined to find a suitable spot.

Although only ten, the girl had been toughened by events few adults had experienced. After leaving Cuba, she had spent many days adrift on a raft with her sister—lost at sea. To be lost in a mangrove jungle? It wasn't a big deal to her.

Sabina wasn't scared. Just mad that Maribel might realize she was gone, and thus have another reason to act superior.

The girl hated the way her older sister would turn her nose up and sigh with disapproval. Most older sisters would shout and threaten. Not Maribel. Maribel never got angry. She never had doubts. She had never been sad enough to write poetry or brave enough to get into trouble. No . . . Maribel was like a princess. She had to be perfect in every way.

Sunlight sprinkled flakes of gold into the shadows.

Sabina pushed on through the brush in a poetic mood—but still angry.

In her head, she imagined a poem she might write:

> *The Princess feasted without care*
> *For a poor, starving girl who dared*
> *To explore a stinking stupid swamp*
> *Alone and unafraid at sea*
> *In search of a private place to stop and . . .*

Abruptly, Sabina abandoned the poem. It was because of what she saw through a gap in the trees. There was an open space where cactus grew among piles of old gray sea-shells. No one around, just tittering birds. The girl battled her way the last few yards toward sunlight.

Finally!

In the clearing was a stump to provide balance. The nearest cactus was a safe distance away. Mosquitoes had stayed behind because they didn't like bright sunlight. That was important. The girl didn't mind bites on her arms and legs, but there were other areas more difficult to scratch.

Yes . . . the perfect spot.

Sabina soon felt comfortable again beneath a circle of clear blue sky. Now all she had to do was find her way back to the boat. But which way was the boat?

The music had either stopped or become too faint to hear. From the other side of the clearing came the sound of water lapping against the shore.

If there was water, maybe the boat was nearby. The girl zigzagged her way through cactus and shells to investigate. As she walked, she noticed a fire pit with a grate for cooking food. Empty cans were strewn around the area. There was a lot of other trash—plywood flats, cigar butts, cellophane, and many beer bottles.

Borrachos, she thought. It was the Spanish word for drunkards. Drunkards had been camping here.

Sabina was sure of it. Beer cans littered a freshly hacked path through the brush. The path angled into a swampy area. She followed the path until a strange buzzing sound caused her to halt. Breathing softly, she tilted her head and strained to listen.

Buzzzzz . . .

The girl took a few more steps and stopped again. Ahead, in a clearing, was a plywood structure. A heavy square shape appeared to be a table. Or was it a beehive? A beehive would explain the loud buzzing she heard. Either way, the structure suggested that the drunkards might still be in the area.

"Hello?" she hollered. Silence made the girl braver, so she demanded, "Why don't you pick up your trash? There is a law against littering—even for drunks."

No answer.

She kept walking. The buzzing grew louder. It was a swarm of flies, not bees, that was making the noise. Thousands of flies. They battled for what looked like chunks of meat spread in rows on a makeshift table.

The girl had seen something similar in Cuba. Fishermen sometimes preserved their catch by laying fish out in the sun to dry. But they were smart enough to cover their fish with salt to keep flies away.

Maybe the drunkards were as sloppy with their food as they were everything else.

Sabina decided to take a closer look—and was horrified by what she discovered. The chunks of "meat" were actually shark fins. Hundreds of them, withered and gray in the heat. The fins resembled wedges of skin from animals that had been killed on a highway.

The girl was furious. "You're criminals—you should all be arrested!" she hollered, confident that the drunkards were gone. Then, at the sound of heavy footsteps, she gulped and crouched low. Someone was sloshing toward her from the water.

"Who's there?" grumbled a man's deep voice.

Sabina crouched lower and touched her necklace of blue and yellow beads. Mangroves blocked her view, but she could see tree limbs thrashing. It was as if a bear were bulling through the mangroves toward the clearing.

Then, a hundred yards away, a dog appeared. It was a large dog with pointed ears. It rippled with muscles beneath brown buckskin fur. The dog stopped as if waiting for its owner. Sabina saw its muscles twitch in the distance. A thick brown nose lifted to sniff the air. The dog's head pivoted . . . and its glowing black eyes found Sabina hiding in the weeds.

At the same instant, from the opposite direction, came the muffled blast of an air horn. Their rental boat was equipped with a horn—a pressurized canister as part of the safety equipment.

Maribel and Luke knew she was gone. They were calling for her.

Sabina got a glimpse of a bearded man exiting the trees. She jumped back, then turned and fled.

Behind her a deep voice ordered the dog, "Get that girl!"

Maribel had the little emergency radio out but was reluctant to call for help. "Sabina might be kicked off our team if they find out she broke the rules," she said to Luke. "I know it's what I should do, but I hate to get her in trouble. And look—"

Her sister had left her inflatable life vest behind— another breach of the rules.

The boy didn't respond. He was staring into the depths of the mangroves. Behind his eyes, the flashing orange light had returned.

Maribel used the air horn again, two piercing blasts. She placed it on the console next to the radio. "I'll go after her. I'm sure Sabina hears us, but she's stubborn. My sister hates to be bossed around. Believe me, that silly girl's not afraid of anything."

Luke continued to stare far into the shadows. The orange light now had a reddish tinge. In his head, a distant sound had been added: the barking of a dog.

"Sabina's already in trouble," the boy said softly.

"I know. I just said that," Maribel replied. "The question is, what should we—"

Luke interrupted. "I'm going after her. You have to stay here." Suddenly he was in a hurry.

"What are you talking about?"

"You're in charge of the boat," the boy reminded her. "You can't leave. That's one of the rules, too, remember?"

Maribel couldn't argue. He was right. But she was also in charge of getting her passengers home safely. "That settles it. I'm calling for help."

She reached for the radio.

"Don't," Luke said. He had removed his gloves for some reason and was reaching for a tree limb. "It wouldn't be the same without your sister when we go fishing."

Maribel started to say, "But she's *my* sister," then stopped and watched the boy swing out of the boat and drop to the ground.

"Luke, you can't," she insisted. "Not by yourself."

Too late. The boy from Ohio was already gone.

The distant drumming of a dog's feet was the most frightening sound Sabina had ever heard. She panicked and ran blindly, screaming for help.

But there was no one to help—not on a deserted island in a clearing of cactus and shells. The girl knew it. She also knew the dog would catch her if she didn't find a way to save herself.

Ahead was the mangrove swamp. Sabina sprinted toward the tallest tree while her eyes scanned the ground for a weapon. She needed something to scare the animal away before it bit her.

Old seashells lay in piles. Some were as large as bricks and just as hard. The girl slowed to scoop up a heavy whelk shell and, after a backward glance, kept running until she was in the shadows of the swamp.

The dog was much closer, coming fast. She got a glimpse of it hurdling a bush, its long, sloppy red tongue drooling. The animal was whining in its eagerness to obey its owner's command:

Get that girl!

When Sabina was frightened, she became angry.

Sometimes that anger clouded her thinking. She stumbled through a curtain of vines to a tree with low, thick limbs. But instead of climbing to safety, she turned and waited. In her hand, she held the seashell like a club.

Not even a dog could run through mangroves, the girl reasoned. It would have to weave its way over and under roots just as she had done. When the animal appeared, Sabina planned to scamper up the tree at the last instant. Maybe even throw the seashell in a half-hearted way.

She didn't want to hurt the dog—just punish it for scaring the wits out of her.

The girl waited for what seemed like a long time but wasn't a long time. She moved away from the tree, then took a few steps toward the clearing, where there was sunlight but no dog that she could see.

Where had it gone?

In the far, far distance someone whistled—a two-finger screech.

She had never heard Luke or Maribel whistle with such ferocity. Had the bearded man called his attack dog home?

The girl stood motionless for what seemed an even

longer period of time but was only a minute. She swatted mosquitoes and waited awhile longer, then decided it was safe to go back to the boat.

Sometimes Sabina's thinking was clouded by anger *and* her impatience.

Which way was the boat?

She didn't know. There hadn't been another blast of an air horn. Fear had blurred her sense of direction. The only way to find her way was to return to the clearing and start over.

Sabina poked her head out from the shadows. The table loaded with shark fins was barely visible in the distance. No sign of the bearded man, either.

Boldly, she stepped into the sunlight and began to jog toward what she hoped was the boat. Then she felt a horrifying chill—to her left, the dog was creeping toward her through the weeds.

On TV, she'd seen lions creep along the ground in the same terrifying fashion. It was their way of surprising smaller animals before they had a chance flee.

Sabina wasn't going to let herself be surprised like those animals. She darted toward the closest tree, but her foot snagged on a vine. She stumbled . . . kept her balance for a few strides . . . then sprawled face-first onto the ground.

The dog's low, thunderous rumble told her to freeze and cover her head. She turned to look anyway, and there the animal was, growling, fangs bared, bounding toward her through weeds.

The girl hurled the whelk and found her necklace of blue and yellow beads. "Make it disappear!" she cried.

The dog snarled and charged . . . then suddenly stopped a few feet away. Its jaws were so close to Sabina's ankles that she felt a gush of hot breath.

At the same instant, a familiar voice startled her from the mangroves. "Don't move," the voice warned. "Act like you're dead."

Luke stepped out and didn't speak another word. Slowly he walked toward the dog. He extended one bare hand like a stop sign—his right hand. The dog barked and lunged, but in a nervous way, as if unsure what to do.

They boy stared into the animal's eyes. He made a downward motion with his hand.

The dog growled and slunk low, intimidated. For an instant, its tail thumped the ground in a friendly way—but the dog bared its teeth when the boy was almost close enough to bite.

Sabina sensed the animal was about the attack. She clutched her beads and yelled, "Make him go away!"

In the far, far distance someone whistled again—a shrill two-finger command.

The dog's ears perked with sudden relief. Its head swiveled to the boy, and a stubby tail once again invited friendship. After Luke made a sweeping motion with his arm, the animal spun around and galloped off.

"My beads saved us," Sabina informed Luke. They were threading their way back to the boat at the time.

Confused, the farm boy rubbed the palm of his right hand. "Your *what* saved us? That's not the way I remember it happening."

The girl wasn't going to repeat details of a story she was eager to share with her sister. So she waited until they were on the boat to say, "I found the shark poacher's camp. He's a disgusting criminal, and his dog's just as bad."

"We've got to tell the police," Maribel said when she had heard the whole story, which included Luke's recollection of events.

"Yes, and have that drunkard arrested," Sabina agreed.

"We'll all be heroes. Even though I'm the one who found the shark poacher—and saved Luke's life."

The boy listened to this in silence. But he did share a rare private look with Maribel, who knew the truth.

Jockeying the boat out of Fools Cut toward the marina was no easier than getting in. It gave Maribel time to realize something: If they notified the police, they would have to tell Hannah and Doc the truth about what Sabina had done. The girl had broken a major rule by leaving the boat without permission. It was possible she would be removed from their shark-tagging team.

"If Doc fires her," Luke said, "he'll have to fire me, too. You told me not to get out of the boat, but I went anyway."

The English word *fire* meant something very different in Spanish. Maribel required a few seconds to understand the boy's meaning. "I'm the one who should be blamed. I'm captain. I'm responsible. So they'll have to fire us all." she said. "What bothers me most is that our mother will be upset when she hears what happened. And she's got enough to worry about."

"They're not going to burn us," Sabina scoffed. "We could make up a story—tell them I saw that drunken criminal while we were fishing." The girl was comfortable with the idea until she realized something: "I don't know, though. I'm the one who should get credit when the police arrest him."

Luke shook his head. He was a terrible liar—always got details mixed up the few times he had tried. "We've got to tell the truth," he said. "Who cares, as long as it stops that guy from netting sharks?"

"The truth," Maribel agreed. "If we don't, Dr. Ford and Hannah will never trust us again."

Sabina was relieved. After daydreaming on the boat trip home, she confirmed the decision by announcing, "I bet we'll become famous. That's what I think. Probably rich, too. They might even interview me on TV."

THIRTEEN
FAME AND SHAME

Later that afternoon the children told their story to Hannah and the biologist. Aside from a stern look or two, there had been no mention of firing anyone or disbanding Sharks Incorporated. In Sabina's opinion, the adults were impressed by how they had handled a dangerous encounter, and eager to have the shark poacher arrested.

"Journalists monitor police radios," Dr. Ford warned after he'd made several phone calls. "Expect reporters to show up about the same time as police. My advice is, ignore them. Wait for a detective friend of mine to get here. His name's J.D. Miller. He wants to talk to you kids alone. That's fine with Hannah, but"—the biologist addressed the sisters—"I'll need to call your mother to get her permission. Is she at home or at work?"

Marta Estéban was at the restaurant, a few miles down the road.

"Don't worry," he added gently. "You kids are heroes. She won't be mad."

Heroes. Sabina loved the sound of that. She sat on a bench with a view of the parking lot. A police car arrived. Next, a plain black car driven by Dr. Ford's detective friend. J.D. Miller was a nice man, big, and wore a sport coat. The man listened patiently to Luke, Maribel, and Sabina describe what had happened. Then he dismissed Sabina, saying, "You can go play now, but don't wander off. It's better, I think, if one of our Spanish-speaking officers takes your statement."

The girl was offended. She was also disappointed. Where were the news reporters the biologist had warned them about?

Half an hour later, it happened. A big fancy van pulled into the parking lot, close to where Sabina was sitting in the shade. From the roof of the van sprouted a huge antenna. The doors opened to reveal a woman dressed for a TV studio, not a warm afternoon at the marina.

The woman was pretty, Sabina decided, especially her glossy crimson high heels and pale pink lipstick. Pinned to the woman's jacket was a tiny microphone. The bag she carried contained what looked like cosmetics and a can of hair spray.

"So you're the one who busted the shark-fin poachers," the woman said to the girl.

"How did you know?" the girl asked.

"Oh, I have my sources," the woman replied. "A police officer friend said that you're a hero. That you, a ten-year-old girl, was responsible for busting some very bad men."

They had retreated to the picnic table near the barbecue grill. Maribel was busy cleaning the rental boat. After speaking to the police detective, Luke had vanished with the dog.

Typical.

Sabina was confused by the word *busting*.

"You mean I broke something? No, *señorita*, when the dog chased me, I fell. I skinned my knee. That's all. Maybe the police will bust that bad man's nose when they find him. I hope so. See them out there?" She pointed toward Fools Cut, where a police boat with flashing blue lights was anchored.

"They're looking for the man now," the girl continued. "I heard that a helicopter might come. If you bring a camera, I bet they'd take us for a ride. Have you ever flown in a helicopter? I haven't, but I'd like to."

The woman had serious eyes but a nice, friendly smile. She leaned across the table to shake hands. "Call me Kathy. I can tell that you are one very brave young lady."

"Yes," Sabina replied. "I know."

The girl's attention strayed to the van. It was white with colorful peacock feathers on the side. "Where's your camera? The detective told me to wait before talking to reporters. Maybe I should. But I'd like to change clothes first and brush my hair."

"You look wonderful," the woman named Kathy said. "This isn't an interview—we're just talking. Why does the detective want you to wait?"

Sabina was reluctant to say but finally admitted, "He wants a police officer who speaks Spanish to talk to me first. He said we—my sister and a boy from a farm named Ohio—he said we shouldn't say anything until the police have collected . . ." The girl paused to think. "I forget the word."

"Evidence?" Kathy asked. "I think you speak English beautifully."

"I think so, too," Sabina agreed. "I've even written a few poems in English, but Spanish is better. It's more musical. English, to me, sounds like coughing. Not singing."

The TV reporter had a notebook open. "Not only brave . . . Sabina Estéban is a young bilingual poet who tags sharks," she murmured, scribbling with a pen. Her smile broadened as she explained, "I'm not interviewing you, understand. Just writing down a few details so I don't forget. Thousands of viewers will want to know everything about you."

Sabina straightened her collar. So far, being famous was fun.

The TV reporter looked up from her notebook. "Is it possible the detective didn't believe your story? I've understood everything you've said so far. Why make you repeat it in Spanish?"

For nearly an hour, the girl had fumed over the same injustice. "It's the way it is in Florida. There are a lot of people who speak English, yet they don't seem to understand English—especially schoolteachers and adults."

"Opinionated, too." The woman chuckled as if she approved. "I think the police are being foolish. That's no reason to doubt an intelligent young lady like yourself. Could there be another reason?"

"The detective didn't like it when I told him I was the only one who saw the shark fins," Sabina admitted. "There should've been another, other uh . . ."

"Witnesses?" the woman suggested. "What about your sister and the boy you mentioned?"

"They stayed in the boat. I didn't mind being lost in the jungle. I'm used to being lost."

"Did you take pictures?" Kathy asked. "Certainly you had your phone with you." The woman held up her iPhone as an example.

"Maybe one day when I'm rich," the girl said, "I'll get a white one just like yours. I wish I'd brought a camera. It was awful—hundreds of shark fins, and so many flies they buzzed like bees. He had a dog, a mean dog—the drunkard I'm talking about. That's the dog that chased me. It might have killed me if I hadn't—"

"Wait," the woman interrupted. "You walked into a mangrove swamp all by yourself—a girl your age? No phone, no way to communicate. Just you, all alone?"

The girl nodded.

"Did you suspect that's where the poachers were hiding?"

Sabina had to give this some thought. "Maybe I did. Yes . . . I think so."

"Then why didn't you turn around and get help?"

"I couldn't," the girl said.

The woman asked, "Because . . . ?" and let the question hang there.

Sabina was embarrassed. She didn't want to discuss the bucket she had refused to use, or her desperate need to go to the bathroom. Not on TV.

"Because I . . . I'm a member of Sharks Incorporated," she said finally. "Our job is to protect sharks, not hurt them."

The reporter named Kathy seemed to accept this. She wanted to know more about their shark-tagging team, then got back to the subject. "When you saw all those shark fins, instead of running away, you went to investigate. Most people, even adults, wouldn't have had the nerve. Are you sure you did this all by yourself?"

"I guess I should have been scared," the girl said, "but I wasn't—until the drunkard ordered his dog to attack me."

"How did you know he was drunk? Did you recognize the man?"

"I will when they arrest him," Sabina replied.

Kathy's pale pink lipstick parted to form a smile. "You sound very sure of yourself."

"I am. The man had a black beard, and there were beer cans everywhere. Don't you hate people who leave trash behind? I would've called the police even if I hadn't seen that table and all those flies buzzing. There must have been a thousand shark fins. Did you know he cuts the fins off while the sharks are still alive?"

The woman, no longer smiling, closed her notebook. "A thousand fins? A moment ago you said hundreds."

"Too many to count," the girl confirmed.

"What makes you think the sharks were still alive when he cut the fins off? Did you speak to the man?"

"Speak to a *drunkard*?" Sabina replied, meaning that speaking to a drunk was a silly thing to do.

"Then how do you know?" the woman insisted. "You just said you would've called the police anyway because of all the trash he'd dumped. Are you sure you actually saw those shark fins? Some might think you were angry about the mess he'd made. That now you're looking for an excuse to have the man arrested."

Without waiting for a response, Kathy leaned closer. "Sabina, let me ask you something. Well, let's put it this way—sometimes when I was a little girl, I made up stories— fun stories. There's nothing wrong with that. But I'm a reporter for a TV station. I also write for the largest news- paper in the area. Do you know what that means?"

Sabina felt her face warming. "Yes, *señorita*, I think so."

"Then tell me, dear. You don't have to make up stories. Just talk to me honestly."

"It means you're rich enough to buy nice shoes and a phone, even though you told lies as a little girl." Sabina said this with an innocence meant to irritate. Then added, "If I was a better liar, maybe I can be rich and famous like you one day."

At first the woman was offended. Then her expression softened. "You've got a big temper for such a little girl."

"I'm not a little girl," Sabina informed her.

"I'm beginning to understand that. You're telling the truth, aren't you?" Kathy's large brown eyes studied the girl intently. "Yes . . . yes, I really think you are. I was foolish to doubt. Don't be mad. Please? I want to be your friend.

Would you like to be interviewed for our news show? I need to speak to your parent or guardian first."

"*Mamá*'s working, but you can call her on the phone," the girl said eagerly.

The reporter asked for the number, then got up, saying, "Excuse me for a second." She walked away from the table with her phone to her ear.

Sabina knew it was rude to eavesdrop. That is why she was good at pretending she wasn't eavesdropping.

The woman had a short, friendly conversation with Mrs. Estéban, then made another call. The reporter seemed to be talking with her boss. She was worried about the time. It was late afternoon. Her story had to be filed in a hurry to make the six o'clock news. For some reason—Sabina didn't understand why—the morning edition of a newspaper might be a better choice.

The police were a concern to Kathy and whomever she was speaking with on the phone. The words *proof* and *evidence* were used several times.

Soon Kathy, motioning to the parking lot, made a third call. A moment later, a man got out of the van. He wore a vest with lots of pockets and lugged a heavy camera toward the picnic table.

"Friends?" the woman asked Sabina, extending her hand again. Her smile had returned.

"Kathy is a such a pretty name," Sabina replied, "and I love your shoes."

After a glance at the woman's bag, which held hair spray and cosmetics, the young girl inquired, "Will you help me put on makeup? Or should I do it myself?"

Luke sensed trouble. He and the dog had found a quiet spot in a shed near the marina parking lot. Through a dusty window was a view of the docks and the picnic table where Sabina was being interviewed.

They had been warned not to talk to reporters. But there was the girl, talking into a microphone, then posing while a female reporter snapped photos with an iPhone.

Earlier, the same woman had focused her phone camera on him and the dog. That is why Luke had taken refuge in a shed piled high with junk and spare engine parts. Now he was tired of hiding.

Pete . . . heel! he thought, and slapped his thigh.

The retriever followed him out the door, across the parking lot. When the reporter called, "Excuse me, Luke . . . can I get a few more pictures?" he kept walking as if he hadn't heard.

His ears were so good, he also heard Sabina say, "Don't bother. He's shy from living with animals. But he is brave—for a farm boy. Did I mentioned he tried to save me from the drunkard's dog?"

For once, the girl was telling the truth about what had happened in the mangroves.

The boy continued walking. He was pleased by Sabina's compliment, yet convinced she was inviting more trouble. He had no idea what kind of trouble. It was a feeling, a small gray cloud in his head.

Later, close to sunset, when the police boat returned to the marina, Luke *knew* he was right.

The detective he'd spoken with, J.D. Miller, was one of five officers who stepped from the boat onto the dock. All the officers wore black ball caps and heavy vests, their guns holstered. The sour look of frustration on their faces told the boy *why* he was right about more trouble.

The reporter and the van were long gone by then.

Luke felt the weight of the detective's eyes as the man walked toward him. The boy turned to the retriever, motioned with his hand, and thought, *Pete . . . swim!*

Pete charged toward the dock and went airborne. Birds scattered. The dog crashed into the water and then surfaced, spouting water from his nose.

Detective Miller approached in a friendly way but appeared tired. "Quite a storm building out there," he said to Luke with a glance to the east. "We were ready to come back anyway—I just wish we'd found something worthwhile."

Every day, over the mainland, heat ricocheted off the ground. It stoked towering clouds of rain and lightning.

"Son," the man added, "I'm afraid I have to ask you a few more questions."

Without thinking, Luke touched the scar on his shoulder and replied, "Yes, sir. I know."

Maribel was concerned when Luke summoned her, and Detective Miller told them, "We searched all through those mangroves. We didn't find any shark fins."

It got worse.

"In fact," the man explained, "we didn't find anything your sister described except two empty beer bottles and the wrapper off a cigar. No trash, no cooking fire. I don't doubt someone was camped there—a path was cut through the mangroves to the water. But here's the thing—"

The detective spread a nautical chart on the picnic table where Sabina had done a television interview and then disappeared. Maribel didn't know where her sister was. Maribel had already explained this to a pair of Spanish-speaking police officers and the detective.

The police officers didn't believe Sabina's story. Maribel was sure of it. One of them had said to the other as they walked away, "These kids just want attention—shark-tagging team, my butt. What a waste of time."

Only Detective Miller seemed willing to believe they weren't liars.

The man leaned over the chart and used a big, thick finger to point. "This is Dinkins Bay. This is the main channel . . . and we're here"—he tapped the table—"at the marina."

His finger moved to a tiny opening on the chart. "This is where we searched—about five acres of swamp and a clearing of high ground. Were we in the right spot?"

The clump of taller mangroves was visible if Maribel looked beyond the docks where boats were moored in a neat line. Luke, sitting to her right, remained silent.

"Fools Cut," she said. "Yes. That's where we were anchored this morning when Sabina got out because she . . . well, my sister needed to use the restroom."

"Fools Cut," the man muttered. "Appropriate. Tell me this—did you see any other boats anchored along here?"

His finger traced the shoreline *inside* the bay.

Luke shook his head. "No, sir. The man and his dog had to have come from the other side of the mangroves."

The detective said, "The guy with the beard, you're talking about? Right?"

Luke nodded.

"But you didn't see him, you said."

Luke replied, "Just his dog. She was part pit bull, I think. She didn't want to bite me, but her owner . . . he must be a real bucket load. When the guy whistled, the dog obeyed right away and took off."

"Bucket load—what's that mean?" the detective wanted to know.

The boy replied, "It's like a, you know, an expression we used on the farm. A bucket load is something you have to scoop up with a shovel. If you call a person a bucket load, I guess it means about the same thing."

Detective Miller tried not to smile. "Never heard it before. Are you sure it was a *female* pit bull?"

Again, the boy nodded. "A nice dog, sort of light brown, with pointed ears and a short tail. She had a thick leather collar with silver things on it. Metal. Like spikes, you know?"

The man gave him an odd look. "A *nice* dog? Let me get this straight. A pit bull attacks you and the little girl, but you liked the dog anyway?"

Luke became defensive. "Of course. It went after Sabina, yeah, then I showed up. You can't blame a dog for obeying a command. She just wanted to please her owner, even if the guy is a real bucket load."

Detective Miller cleared his throat as if about to deliver more bad news.

"Here's the problem," he said, addressing Maribel. "Whoever camped there wasn't a poacher—at least, there's no evidence we could find. And I seriously doubt your sister saw several hundred shark fins drying in the sun. To catch that many sharks, you'd need a fairly large boat, wouldn't you?"

Maribel felt as if she were walking into a trap, but she had to agree. "Probably . . . yes. A boat a lot bigger than the one we've been using."

"Then it didn't happen," the detective said. "It couldn't have happened—not the way your sister described it."

"My sister wouldn't lie," Maribel responded. She might have spoken more forcefully if Sabina hadn't invented so many wild stories in the past.

"I'm not saying she did," the man assured her. "Where the guy was camped, it's almost all swamp. It's easy to get turned around, and for a kid her age to imagine all sorts of things. Take a look—here's why I'm sure that shark poachers weren't camped there."

He tapped the chart and traced the shoreline *outside* the bay. "Do you see what I'm getting at?"

Luke understood. "The chart says the water's too shallow there for a big boat to get in. Is that what you're saying?"

"Too shallow even for a small boat," the man said. "If someone anchored on that side of the mangroves, they had to be in a canoe. A kayak, maybe. Every fishing guide I spoke with agrees.

"There's a big sandbar close to the trees," he continued.

"We didn't find any footprints in the sand, nothing to indicate that poachers anchored in deeper water and waded ashore. Can you imagine trying to swim carrying a table and a hundred pounds of shark fins?"

For the first time, Maribel began to doubt her sister's story.

Luke did not. "That man was poaching sharks," he insisted softly. "If Sabina hadn't seen a table full of fins, the man wouldn't have told his dog to attack her."

"You have a point . . . but I think you're wrong," Detective Miller said. He was folding the chart, done with questions. "Just in case, whatever you do, don't talk to any reporters. Okay?"

Maribel came close to confessing that Sabina already had spoken to a reporter. But instead she asked, "Why not?"

The detective explained, "For your own safety. The bearded guy was probably just camping, but . . . well, if Luke's right, you don't want a band of poachers to see your pictures in the paper. And you certainly don't want them to read your names or find out where you live."

"A band of poachers," Luke said. "You mean, like a whole gang?"

"We've been after them for almost a month," the detective said. "They've been operating between Tampa Bay and Marco Island, and it's always the same. We'll find a bunch of dead sharks, their fins cut off, so we send out patrol boats, even helicopters. Day and night, we've searched for this gang. But we've yet to even see them, let alone arrest them."

The man sighed with frustration. "Kids, it's a mystery to me. These poachers are smart—and that's exactly why I don't want you talking to reporters. Criminals can be bullies. Sneaky, too. Sometimes they'll confront a witness, thinking it'll keep them out of jail."

"Confront how?" Maribel asked.

The detective didn't answer. But the way he shook his head warned, *You don't want to find out.* "Stay close to the marina," he said. "Don't go anywhere without an adult along. I've got a business card here somewhere." He fumbled for an inside pocket. "That's my cell number. Call me if you need something."

Maribel fretted about the warning. She was also worried about the TV interview that Sabina had done. When the detective was gone, she tried to reassure herself by discussing it with Luke. "The police don't believe Sabina, so why would a TV reporter believe her? They can't run a story without proof, can they?"

Luke's attention had turned inward. "Instead of talking you into fishing Fools Cut, I should have talked you out of it," he said. "It's my fault. I knew something bad would happen if we went there."

"That's just silly," Maribel said. "There's no way you could've known that Sabina would wander off and get lost. What I think is"—she reached as if to touch the boy's arm but didn't—"you're even worse than me when it comes to blaming yourself. And I . . . well, I think you're one of the nicest boys I've ever met."

"But I *did* know," Luke insisted, his voice soft.

Towering clouds in the east provided a thoughtful silence. A smoky haze beyond the mangroves was rain. The sky throbbed with colors, green and purple. Clouds lit the bay with a sudden, silent bolt of distant lightning.

The boy began tugging at the fingers of his right hand to remove the glove. "Maribel . . . there's something I should have told you. And showed you. Sabina tried to trick me into doing it, but I wouldn't."

The girl watched in silence as Luke paused, unsure. "What's wrong?" she asked. "There's nothing you can't tell me. Luke, don't you feel like you and I are"—the girl sensed her face reddening—"well, that we're . . ." She couldn't say what she wanted to say, so she finished shyly, "After all, we're teammates, aren't we?"

Luke hated discussing anything personal. "I'd better get going," he decided, no longer tugging at the glove. "Doc's got some heavy boxes he needs moved."

The boy whistled for the dog and walked away.

FOURTEEN
NO NEWS IS GOOD NEWS

Sabina had gone to a lot of trouble to watch the six o'clock news after Kathy, the news reporter, and the TV van packed up and left. That's why the girl was close to tears when she returned to the marina on a bicycle that wasn't hers to use, or even borrow.

Maribel was waiting on the lower deck of their houseboat.

"What's wrong, dear?" she asked.

"Leave me alone," the younger sister snapped.

"Sabina, please, at least listen! The detective had more questions. There were a couple of Spanish-speaking officers, too. We looked all over for you—and there's a storm coming. What if Detective Miller finds out you left on a stolen bicycle?"

"I bet that would make you happy!" Sabina responded. "Put me in jail, where I belong. Leave me all alone with rats and no food. Soon I'll be so old I won't care anymore about owning a television or a bicycle. Or even my own cell phone."

The girl pushed past her sister. She went into her closet-sized room and slammed the door.

Maribel had weathered these tantrums before.

On the stove, beans simmered. The older girl went back to work, draining the rice and setting it aside to cool. Captain Hannah had provided four nice sea trout fillets for dinner. The fillets were thin and white as piecrust. They would take only a few minutes to cook.

Their mother, who was convinced her daughters were being hailed as heroes, not liars, was working and wouldn't be home until late. On the phone, Mrs. Estéban had promised to return with a surprise of some sort—probably carrot cake, their favorite dessert.

But making tonight's dinner, and keeping her sister out of trouble, was still Maribel's responsibility.

The houseboat was like an oversized dollhouse with

miniature appliances. There was a two-burner stove and a minifridge that fit under the counter. The refrigerator was small but never empty. Maribel loaded a plate with mango cobbler and tapped on Sabina's door.

"Go away!" the girl yelled from inside. "I'm trying to finish a poem before the police handcuff me."

The older sister opened the door just wide enough to stick her arm in. The plate of cobbler was snatched from her hand. As she walked away, the door banged shut, then opened again. "Where's the milk?" Sabina hollered down the hall. "Don't tell me we can't afford milk, either!"

Maribel returned with a glass of milk. She tapped twice and then left it outside the door.

Thunder rumbled across the bay while the girl set the table. It was raining, almost dark, when she lit a burner and found a pan for the sea trout.

The phone on the wall rang. Their mother always called just before dinner if the girls were home alone.

"Everything's fine, *mamá*," Maribel said, as she always did—no matter what small calamity had occurred. Why upset their mother when she had enough problems to deal with? Through the phone Maribel heard the background sounds of laughter and clattering plates in a restaurant. The place was always crowded with customers who liked to sit and watch a dozen big-screen TVs on the walls.

Maribel and her mother talked for a while in Spanish before their mother mentioned Sabina. "Your sister was here earlier," Mrs. Estéban said. "I saw her peeking through the window. I think Sabina came to watch the six o'clock news. Is she okay?"

"She's in her room writing poetry," Maribel replied. "I figured that's where she went. She was crying when she got home, but she's fine now. She ate a plate of cobbler and asked for a glass of milk."

"That poor sweet child," their mother said. "I wish I could have given her a hug, but I was busy with my tables. Did she tell you? That TV reporter didn't use her interview. Your sister waited and waited, then finally gave up. I know she's disappointed."

Maribel, with a gentle smile, said, "I figured that out, too."

"It makes me sick to think about that bad man and dog chasing her," their mother continued. "Honestly? I'm glad Sabina wasn't on the news tonight. Who knows what that criminal would do if he saw her."

In the background, above the noise of clattering plates, a voice called her mother's name. "I've got to go," Mrs. Estéban said, then added in a sweet way, "You and Sabina will always be heroes to me—*mi pequeña general*."

The next morning, a Friday, Luke wondered why there was a school bus in the marina parking lot. During summer vacation? That made no sense.

He and the dog continued walking toward the lab. When he got closer, he saw *Everglades Sea Camp* written on the side of the bus. So maybe it did make sense. Luke had never attended a summer camp. How could he, with so many chores to do on the farm? But he had read about summer camps, which is why he found the presence of the bus interesting. He stopped to watch.

The bus doors folded open. A bunch of kids filed off, all wearing the same green summer camp T-shirts. There was a mix of girls and boys. They looked to be a little older than Luke, probably thirteen years old.

"Hey . . . there he is!" a girl shouted. Then, for some

mysterious reason, she pointed in Luke's direction. The girl, he couldn't help but notice, was tall and sort of pretty. She sounded excited, like she had spotted a celebrity.

Curious, Luke turned a slow circle to see who the girl was talking about. But there was no one else there. Just him.

"He's the one who scared off the pit bull," the girl hollered. She held up a newspaper for the other kids to see. "It *is* him. Look for yourself. Hey," she called to Luke. "Mind if I get a selfie?"

A taller, older boy, chimed in, "Dude—mind if I get one, too?"

The girl, getting her phone out, loped toward Luke as if she wanted to be the first in line.

Luke felt dazed. It took him a moment to solve this strange mystery. He remembered the TV reporter. He remembered her iPhone camera. Had the woman published a picture of him in the newspaper? No . . . that wasn't possible. He had refused to say a word to her or anyone else.

But that's exactly what had happened.

"Your name's Luke, isn't it?" the girl called as she jogged closer. "Says so right here." She motioned with the newspaper. "Please, just a couple of selfies. And maybe autograph your picture from the newspaper—just for me. Okay?"

Luke tried to get his clumsy feet moving, but they felt mired in glue. "I . . . I can't," he stammered.

Too late. The girl was already there. She threw an arm around the boy's shoulder and pressed her cheek against his ear.

"Smile, Luke." She laughed, looking up at her phone. *Click, click, click.* Several selfies were snapped while Luke stood frozen. Finally, after a very damp kiss on the cheek, the girl pulled away. "If our counselor says it's okay, could you hang with us for a while? I'd love to hear what it's like to tag sharks. All we do at this stupid camp is collect starfish and shells—kiddie stuff like that."

Luke, rubbing his cheek, said, "Uh . . . I've got to go."

And he did—walking at first. Then began to jog.

Sabina was still in a foul mood when she left the houseboat that morning. She didn't notice that the air was fresh and tangy after last night's rain. She didn't notice when people in neighboring boats smiled and waved at her with new admiration. When a pair of marina employees, Jeth and Figgy, applauded as she walked past, the girl ignored them with a scowl.

It was bad enough to have been scorned by yesterday's six o'clock news. Now people were making fun of her because she had hoped to become famous but wasn't.

Sabina's mood didn't improve when she spotted Luke in the distance. He was in the parking lot with a bunch of older kids. Among them was a tall, pretty girl. The young pig farmer didn't seem to mind one bit when the girl hugged him close. Then he stood there like a dumb statue, cheek-to-cheek as if kissing the girl while several selfies were taken. Or did he mind . . . ?

Sabina watched Luke finally pull free of the girl's arms. For an instant the boy paused with a stupid grin frozen on his face. Then, at a fast pace, he started walking toward a fence at the edge of the parking area. The pretty girl, with her even stupider grin, trotted after him, along with several other kids.

The young pig farmer, Sabina noticed, glanced once over his shoulder. When he realized the girl was following him, he sprinted away as if running for his life.

Sabina knew where the boy was headed—to a shed filled with junk, where he sometimes hid when he didn't want to talk to anyone. She also knew a shortcut. She bolted past the boat ramp, through a hole in the fence, and was waiting in the shed when Luke arrived.

"Sure, take selfies and kiss strange girls while the rest of us are working," she sneered from the darkness as the boy entered.

Luke was so startled he stumbled and nearly fell. "Holy moly!" he yelped. "You scared the whiz out of me. I thought you were . . . that you were . . ."

"Thought I was that girl with her stupid grin and cell phone?" Sabina demanded. "You'd like that, wouldn't you? Have someone pretty take my place on the boat while I'm busy making your gross bologna sandwiches. Maybe next time I won't save you from a mean dog."

"Save *me*?" Luke said. He felt a little dizzy. "What are you doing here?" He held up a warning finger. "Hang on a second." He scooted along the wall to a broken window and peeked out. "Good. She's gone. Uh, that was so freaky. She wet-*kissed me*. Like cows do sometimes?" The boy scratched at his cheek as if trying to remove a stain.

"Hah—don't change the subject," Sabina countered. "And don't think I won't tell Maribel. I will, and she won't like it. Personally, I don't care who you kiss . . . as long as it's not me. But you're supposed to be grinding fish for chum, not flirting with—" The sister stopped, aware that something was missing. "Hey—where's Marion's dog?"

"Doc's dog?" Luke risked another glance out the window. "How the heck would I know? Swimming, probably." He scratched at his cheek again. "Wow. That girl's scary—maybe she scared the dog away, too."

Sabina thought the remark funny until the boy became very serious. "You know why she wanted to take selfies with me? Because she saw my picture in the paper and wanted an autograph."

"Now you're making up stories," the girl scoffed. "Next, cows will be asking for your autograph."

"Sabina, it's true about the picture. We're in trouble. *Bad* trouble. Detective Miller isn't going to like it. Doc and my aunt, they're all going to be mad when they find out."

"I don't blame them," Sabina said, "if they saw you kissing a stranger in the—" Again, she stopped. "What picture? I hate that girl. Why would a pretty girl want your autograph?"

"Because of you. You haven't seen today's newspaper?"

"Paper?" the girl asked. "How would I? We can't afford a newspaper."

Like a criminal, Luke ducked under the window and

moved to the doorway. "This really sucks," he said. "I didn't read the story, but I saw it. Your picture's on the front page, too. Right beside mine." He tilted his head for a quick look out the door. "Holy moly, those girls are still out there waiting."

Sabina was stunned by what she had just heard. "Newspaper . . . Me?"

"Yeah. And your picture's a lot bigger than mine."

A slow smile brightened the girl's face. "On the front page . . . and it's even bigger than yours," she mused.

"You should've never talked to that reporter," Luke said. "This is bad. Strangers from all over the place are going to be stopping us and asking questions. And what if that bearded guy, the shark poacher, sees it?"

"Oh, yes. That would be bad," Sabina agreed, but she was excited, not upset. "Where can I find this newspaper? I'd like to see the terrible thing I've done."

When Mrs. Estéban finished reading about her daughters and their friend, Luke, there were tears in the woman's eyes.

She folded the newspaper carefully and said to Maribel, "Take this back to the marina. I'll give you some money. We'll want several copies to keep for your scrapbooks. But I'm scared that criminal will see Sabina's picture. Please don't tell her that I'm worried."

"Don't be, *mamá*," Maribel said. "The police will find the man. And who's going to bother us here? The marina has a gate they lock every night."

Mrs. Estéban sniffed and went to find her purse. "I'm so proud of my two girls," she said from the hallway. "Maribel, you especially. I'm glad the reporter didn't interview you, too. But she should've. You were captain of the boat."

Maribel didn't want to cause more upset by mentioning the detective's warning about reporters. "I don't mind," the girl said. She stopped at the counter and opened the paper for another look.

On the front page, Sabina's smile was so broad it revealed the missing front tooth that had yet to grow back. Her sister looked happy and fearless in her dark blue Sharks Incorporated T-shirt.

Sabina looks exactly like herself, Maribel thought fondly. *She's so beautiful but doesn't know it yet.*

The photo of Luke and the dog was different. In person,

Luke was an average-looking boy. He had a wide, plain face, reddish hair, and shy, soft eyes. But the camera had sharpened the boy's features. Somehow the picture made Luke appear larger, more confident. The lens had captured a spark in his bright blue eyes, not shy at all—a little angry, even, at the reporter for taking his photo.

The spark was unusually bright. Maribel wondered if using a magnifying glass to look at the picture would confirm that it resembled a lightning bolt.

"Buy at least five copies," her mother said, and handed over a ten-dollar bill. She put her arm around the girl, and they both gazed at the front page. "What worries me is this part. What if that terrible man sees it?" The woman circled a paragraph with her finger. It was midway down in the story.

The paragraph read:

Sabina Estéban, the youngest of the three team members, feels confident she can identify the shark poacher. She described him to police in detail, as well as the man's trained pit bull. The girl claims the dog attacked her. She says it might have bit her had it not been for the bravery of her fellow shark tagger, Lucas O. Jones.

Lucas was unavailable for comment . . .

"My English isn't as good as yours," her mother said. "I'm not sure I understand what some of those words mean."

Inside the houseboat they spoke Spanish, so Maribel translated the paragraph line by line.

"That Sabina." Her mother smiled. "She's not afraid of anything. Even as a baby she was . . . different. Born old, the women in white used to say of her in Cuba. And the *women in white* are very wise. Yes . . . your sister worries me most of all."

Maribel thought, *Me too.*

She gave her mother a hug and said, "I'll be back with the newspapers and your change."

Outside, she noticed Luke. The boy was peering through a hole in the fence that separated the parking lot from a junky area where there were broken engines and a machine shed.

"Where's my sister?" Maribel asked.

"Went to buy a newspaper at the general store," Luke replied. "I told her not to go alone."

"Why shouldn't she go alone?" To Maribel, Sanibel Island felt like the safest place in the world. At this time of day, they were allowed to roam freely. And Bailey's General

Store was only a few hundred yards from the shell road that led to the marina. It was an easy walk.

Luke replied, "For the same reason Detective Miller told us not to talk to reporters."

A stricken look crossed Maribel's face but quickly faded. "I'm sure she'll be fine. There are always people on the bike path between here and Bailey's."

Luke had another reason for being concerned. He pointed to the parking lot. "Ever see that van before? It pulled in just before your sister left. Now it's . . . yeah, looks like they're leaving. I've got a weird feeling about the driver."

He was referring to a beat-up old black van with black tinted windows. Exhaust spewed from its tailpipe as the vehicle pulled away.

Maribel began to worry again. "Is Sabina walking, or did she borrow someone's bike?"

"Walking," Luke said. He touched the girl's elbow. "Come on. Let's go find her." In the parking lot, he stopped again. "Hold on. That darn bus is still here."

Now the boy was concerned about a yellow school bus with *Everglades Sea Camp* on the side.

Maribel gave him a quizzical look. "What's wrong with

you? Why were you peeking through the fence like a criminal a little bit ago?"

She figured it out when a tall, pretty girl and several other kids exited the marina office and came toward them. They grinned and waved while the tall girl yelled, "Come on, Luke, hang for a while. Seriously, like, everyone on the bus wants a selfie with you."

FIFTEEN
MIRRORS AND THE BLACK VAN

Sabina didn't notice the black van when it passed by. She was preoccupied. It wasn't easy to walk and read a newspaper at the same time. The excitement of seeing her own smiling face on the front page made her giddy.

I look sort of pretty, she thought. *Prettier than I look in the mirrors at home.*

Could this be possible? The girl stopped on the bike path to study the photograph. Yes . . . it was true. And if the reporter with the pink lipstick, Kathy, hadn't been so stingy about sharing makeup, the photo might have been even more glamorous.

Sabina searched her own dark eyes. She liked the simple eloquence of her braided hair in the photo. Her blue-black braids framed what she deemed to be a friendly, confident smile. The only small flaw was her missing front tooth, knocked out by a baseball.

So what? The tooth would grow back, Sabina hoped, in time for the attractive and successful woman that the photo promised she would one day become.

I like photographs better than mirrors, she decided. *I will never trust a mirror again.*

The girl continued walking. Behind her on the road, a black van with black tinted windows slowed, then crept past.

This time the girl did notice. The engine made a clunky metallic sound and spit gray exhaust. The odor tainted the fresh, tangy morning air.

This reminded her of Cuba, and the old, brightly colored American cars that stank up the streets of Havana.

Use a bicycle, she advised the driver silently. *Stop polluting our air.*

Her attention returned to the newspaper. The article was in English, of course. People in Florida—kids at school, especially—didn't realize it took time to understand a new language. There was a difference between learning a language and understanding it. There was also a difference between speaking a language and being able to read it without having to squint, and think, and sometimes feel stupid.

Sabina was reading the story when the van reappeared. This time, instead of passing by, the vehicle pulled off the road and stopped next to her.

A front window glided down. The woman at the wheel said, "Hey, you're the little girl in the newspaper, aren't you? We were just talking about you." After looking the girl up and down, she added, "My gracious. You're even prettier in person."

The woman had nice hair and a waxy red smile.

"I think so, too," Sabina replied in a friendly way.

"Do you live nearby?" the driver asked.

The girl pointed at the shell road that led to the marina. "On a houseboat," she said. "Uh, do you mind if I ask you something? Where you live, why do they allow junky cars that stink up the air with pollution?"

The woman didn't understand. She spoke to someone in the back seat, asking for the newspaper and a pen. "I'd love to have your autograph," she said to Sabina. "I bet you're tired of folks telling you how brave you are to stand up to those criminals. Weren't you scared?"

Sabina shrugged as if it was no big deal. "I hate anyone

who kills sharks for no reason. I'm a member of a shark-tagging team—it's probably in the story you read about me. I haven't gotten that far yet because it's hard to walk and read at the same time." With a regal nod, the girl added, "After I autograph your newspaper, you may take my picture if you want."

The van's windows were tinted black. Sabina couldn't tell how many passengers were seated behind the woman. Soon the woman's copy of the newspaper was provided from the back seat by a man's large, hairy hand.

"I bet you're tired of signing autographs, too," the woman said. She held out the newspaper for the girl to take.

Sabina walked closer to the van and extended her hand. "I'll never get tired of signing autographs."

The newspaper was already folded to the front page. Concentrating, tongue pressed between her teeth, the girl signed the photo with a flourish. This was something that Sabina had practiced many times in her room alone. She also granted the woman a patient smile, which she had seen in magazines. Movie stars did this to prove they were nice people even though they were rich.

"Thank you," she said to the woman, and got up on

her toes to return the newspaper. As she did, the girl got a quick glimpse of the passenger in the back seat.

It was a big, thick-faced man with a short dark beard.

There was a dog there, too. Sabina couldn't see the dog, but its low rumbling growl sounded familiar. The stink of cigar smoke escaped from inside. That was familiar, too.

Sabina backed away.

"What's wrong?" the woman asked.

The girl suddenly found it hard to breathe. She spun and almost ran in the wrong direction. But then she saw her sister and Luke coming toward her from the road to the marina.

Concerned, the woman opened the car door. "What about our picture together?" she wanted to know. "Honey . . . you're as white as a sheet. Is something wrong?"

Sabina started running. She didn't stop until she was at Maribel's side. "It's him . . . It's the shark poacher," she stammered, out of breath.

Maribel's eyes narrowed. "Are you sure?" she asked, aware that the van was pulling away. Not fast, but cautiously, as if not to attract attention.

"He had a beard, and his dog growled at me," Sabina

stammered. "We've got to call the police before he gets away."

Luke covered his eyes against the sun's glare. "Don't worry, I can see the license plate."

"From *here*?" Maribel asked. It shouldn't have surprised her, but it did. Luke, the boy with the bionic eyes. "Then we need to write the number down before you forget."

Luke didn't need to write it down. The license plate had become a photograph in his head.

He turned to Sabina. "Are you sure it's the same guy? What about the dog? Did you get a good look at the dog?"

Sabina watched the van stop at a stop sign and turn right.

"I think so," she said. Then decided, "Yes . . . I'm sure it was the shark poacher. We've got to call Detective Miller!"

Luke said it wasn't too late in the day to fish, yet he had to admit that Maribel was right: They couldn't leave the marina until the police had located the black van. It wasn't safe. Also, once the police did find the van, they might call upon Sabina to identify the passenger as the man who had ordered a pit bull to attack her.

Identifying the dog—if there was a dog—would require Luke to be present, too.

So the boy had some time to waste. He got one of the heavy fishing rods they used, and practiced casting off the dock. Luke seldom gave himself credit for much, but after weeks of practice, even he had to admit that he was getting pretty good. The rod was seven feet long. Despite the heavy line, he could whip a bait with pinpoint accuracy. Casting sticks for the dog had improved his distance, too. On a baseball diamond, Luke could throw from home to second base, no problem. With a fishing rod, he could hurl a weighted line almost twice as far.

Fun.

When he was done, he put the rod away and strolled to the lab. The retriever was swimming beneath the docks when he arrived. The biologist's boat was gone. This wasn't unusual. But Luke was surprised when his aunt Hannah told him that Doc had left unexpectedly on a trip.

"I saw that he'd moved his seaplane," the boy said. "Where'd he go?"

They were in the lab. The room smelled of chemicals

and saltwater. Against the wall, the row of aquariums bubbled while ceiling fans stirred a lazy breeze.

Hannah didn't know. Nor did she know when the biologist was returning.

"It's the way Doc is," she explained. "His job comes first. It's the same with me and my charter business—except for Izaak, of course. Doc and I are both learning to accept the way we are. Sometimes he's gone for a week or two—or longer. No one knows until he gets back."

Luke was disappointed. He'd felt a connection with the biologist that, for him, was unusual. He also feared he had let the man down by failing in his duties as "special lookout" for their team. It was his fault they had decided to fish in Fools Cut.

Hannah sensed this. "It's possible that Doc wouldn't have left unless he trusted you to take care of yourself. Ever think of that?"

No . . . just the opposite. Luke's stepfather, even his teachers back in Ohio, had criticized almost everything he did. The idea of an adult actually trusting him was still new.

The woman continued, "Something I know for sure is, I wouldn't let the three of you tag sharks if I didn't trust you all. But there is something that bothers me."

Luke expected her to ask yet again why Sabina had been allowed to leave the boat to go to the bathroom rather than use a bucket. Maribel had taken the blame to protect her sister. The boy had backed this white lie because . . . well, because they really were a team.

Instead, Hannah asked, "Do you think Sabina's right about who she saw in the van? The police were willing to believe her once. They spent half a day searching those mangroves but didn't find any evidence of shark poachers. Now Sabina's doing it again: accusing a man of a serious crime, even though she only got a quick glimpse of the guy. What if they stop the van and she's wrong?"

Luke understood. "If that happens, the police probably won't ever believe us again. I see what you're getting at."

Hannah was tall, with dark hair and sharp, wise eyes. Fishing guides also had to be tough. Hannah was. "That's what bothers me. What happens if you and the sisters really do get in trouble? Call for help a third time, the police won't come running. Honestly, Luke, I wouldn't blame them."

His aunt paced awhile to think things through. "That's bad. It would create a safety risk. Doc and I discussed it before he left. If Sabina has made up another story, and the police prove her wrong, I'm afraid it means the end of Sharks Incorporated. Either that, or you and Maribel have to tell her she can't fish anymore. Sorry, but that's the way it has to be."

"We're not fishing without Sabina," Luke replied softly. "Don't worry about her. She's telling the truth."

"You sound sure."

"I am. Sabina's sort of weird and all, with her lucky beads and poetry, but she's no liar. She wouldn't risk messing up our chance to tag sharks together."

"Loyalty is a great quality," Hannah said. "But how do you know she didn't imagine it all? Sabina's a, uh . . . creative girl. Sort of theatrical, I'd say."

The boy couldn't explain how or why he knew, but he *knew*. It had something to do with how his brain worked since being struck by lightning. Or had he really changed? That's why he'd come to the lab. He wanted to discuss the subject with Doc, a man who could be trusted not to send him back to a hospital for more tests, more brain scans. But now the biologist was gone.

"You'll see," Luke said. "When the police find the van, I'll recognize the guy's pit bull, and his dog will recognize me. I guarantee it. That'll prove Sabina has been telling the truth all along."

Hannah, smiling, seemed to accept that. "Then I believe in Sabina, too. But there's something else to consider. If police find the van, and Sabina's right, have you thought about what will happen next?"

No, but it seemed obvious to the boy. "They'll arrest the guy, I suppose, and the rest of his gang. If there is a gang. The only thing that worries me is, what'll happen to his dog?"

"That's not all," Hannah said. "You haven't heard the news?"

Uh-oh, Luke thought. "Maribel and I haven't talked to any reporters. What news?"

"Yesterday afternoon, the Ocean Environmental Association offered a reward for help in arresting the shark poachers. It was on local TV." Hannah let that sink in before adding, "Fifty thousand dollars, Luke."

The boy gulped.

"If Sabina's right, and they arrest the man she saw, it won't just be local news," Hannah said. "It'll be all over the internet. Reporters will come looking for the kids who busted what police think is the largest poaching ring in Florida. You'll be famous for a while. Sharks Incorporated will make headlines."

After waiting in silence for a response, the woman confided, "I know what happened today. You were swarmed by a busload of teenage fans—one girl in particular. How did it feel to be a celebrity?"

"Sabina loves that stuff," the boy replied. "Maribel, not so much. And me—" He grimaced, meaning he hated the attention.

"You don't like being pursued by a girl who wants to get to know you better? I not only saw her, I talked to her for a while. I thought she was very nice. There's nothing wrong with meeting new people. But new friends aren't nearly as important as old friends you can share your secrets with."

He wondered if his aunt was referring to Maribel and Sabina.

"What did the girl say?" he asked.

"The one in the parking lot? She wanted to get to know you better. And something about just hanging for a while. But you took off, which sort of reminds me of how Marion would've handled the situation."

Luke took that as a compliment until he noticed the odd, bittersweet smile on his aunt's face. "What do you mean?"

Hannah, joking but serious, too, said, "Doc runs away if someone tries to get too close. A lot of people do. If that girl decides to try again, I think you ought to ask yourself, what are you *really* running from?"

Thankfully, the laboratory phone rang. Hannah answered, saying, "Sanibel Biological Supply."

It was the name of Dr. Ford's business.

Luke was trying to slip out the door unnoticed when Hannah stopped him.

"The police found the black van," she said. "Detective Miller is on his way. He wants to talk to all three of you."

"I guess we won't be fishing for sharks today," the boy responded.

The woman nodded in a way that was unusually serious. "Probably not," she said, not smiling.

SIXTEEN
THE WRONG MAN

Today, Detective Miller wasn't dressed to slog through mangrove swamps. He carried a briefcase and wore slacks and a gray shirt, the collar unbuttoned. It was a hot afternoon in June. He sat on one side of a picnic table. Maribel, Sabina, and Luke sat on the other side, facing him, while Captain Hannah stood. It was the only shady spot around, thanks to coconut palms that circled the area.

"I can't question you officially without a parent or guardian present," he said. "So it's up to you. I spoke to your mother, Sabina. She said it's okay if we have a private talk. Just between us. How does that sound, Maribel?"

"Fine," the older sister said, yet she was unsettled by the man's grave manner.

Hannah decided it was time to leave the kids on their own. "Holler if you need me," she said. Before walking toward the dock where her boat was tied, she gave the detective a private, knowing look.

Luke thought, *They're both trying to protect us from something.*

The detective attempted to put them at ease by mentioning yesterday's newspaper article. He didn't sound upset.

"I liked the picture of you, Sabina. You too, Luke. The reporter wanted to interview me, but by the time I returned her call, it was too late. Thing is," he said, "I don't think the story would've run if the reporter had known the truth—we didn't find the shark fins or any poachers. No evidence at all. Would you have been disappointed if your pictures weren't in the paper?"

He looked at Sabina when he asked the question.

"Of course," the girl said. "Who wouldn't want to see their picture on the front page?"

This answer was not unexpected.

"I bet you'd like to be on TV, too, huh?" the man suggested. "Have reporters waiting in line. Or appear on talk shows in a nice studio in front of cameras? If you helped put a gang of shark poachers in jail, your picture would be all over the internet. We're talking worldwide, not just Florida. You might even get the reward the Ocean Environmental Association has offered."

"Reward?" Sabina's eyes widened. Neither Luke nor Hannah had mentioned the reward. "How much?" she asked. "Is a television crew on their way? Then I should change my clothes if—"

The weight of Maribel's hand on her arm silenced the girl.

The detective's voice grew softer. "No, no reporters are coming this time. And there will be no reward. I guess every kid daydreams about being rich and famous. There's nothing wrong with that. Problem is, Sabina, it is wrong to accuse a person of something without proof. In fact, it's a crime. I'm talking about the black van we stopped an hour ago."

Sabina knew that police had found the van. She had expected good news, not this. "A . . . a crime?" The girl felt a prickly sensation down her spine. "But I didn't do anything wrong."

Detective Miller said, "Let's make sure you don't. You could get into a lot of trouble if you accuse the gentleman who owns the van of ordering his dog to attack you. There'd be paperwork. If he's willing to cooperate, we'd arrange for you get a good look at him without him seeing you. But if he refused, we'd have to get a court order—all based on the story you told us."

The detective opened his briefcase while he continued talking. "The gentleman and his daughter might not like that. Of course, it wouldn't matter if he really is the one who tried to hurt you. But if you're wrong, Sabina, they might press charges. I'm not saying they would, but it's possible. That's why I wanted to speak with you kids privately. I want you to see something."

He removed a laptop and positioned it front of the girl. Luke and Maribel got up so they could look over Sabina's shoulder.

"My car's equipped with a dashcam," the detective said. "This is video of what happened when we stopped the gentleman's van. I can freeze it or replay a section anytime you want. Don't be shy. Then you have to decide whether to press charges or not."

"What does this mean, 'press charges'?" the girl wanted to know.

Maribel had never felt so nervous. "It's your chance

to see if it's the same man," she explained to her sister in Spanish. "But you have to be one hundred percent certain. Understand? *Please*—no more stories just to get your photograph in newspapers."

Sabina responded with three sharp words in Spanish.

Luke had heard these words before, so he wasn't surprised when Maribel scolded, "Stop your swearing and pay attention! This is serious."

The younger sister, teeth clenched, folded her arms. She sat like a statue while the detective touched the laptop. The police dashcam video came to life on the screen.

It was the same black van with black tinted windows. Luke recognized the license plate. Watching was like sitting in the front seat with Detective Miller. The van, spewing exhaust, slowed and pulled over in a grassy area. It wasn't a busy road. Another police car arrived, blue lights flashing. Moments later, a third police car swerved in as if to block the van's escape.

Luke felt his stomach tense. He began to realize how much work the police had done to investigate Sabina's claims.

The detective appeared on the screen with his back to the camera. He walked to the van and spoke to whoever was driving. The angle wasn't good, and there was no sound. Their conversation went on for a while.

The detective stepped away and opened the van's side door. Automatically, a metal ramp folded out. Two officers in uniform joined him. Together, they helped someone in a wheelchair down the ramp and onto the grass beside the road.

The officers were big men. Their bodies screened the wheelchair from view.

The van's driver-side door opened. When a woman got out, the detective reached across the picnic table and stopped the video.

"Is that the woman who asked for your autograph?" he asked Sabina.

The girl was no longer a statue. She sat slumped, with her hands in her lap, and answered meekly. "Yes. I thought she was nice until I saw the man behind her. Why does she look so scared? And she's . . . is she crying?"

"Can you blame her?" Detective Miller responded. "According to her, all she wanted was your autograph and maybe a picture. She said you ran away for no reason. That you were upset, and she got out and offered to help. Is that true?"

"I don't know . . . I thought she might try to grab me, so I—" The girl stopped and got control of herself. "I'm telling the truth!" she insisted. "Where's the man, and the dog that growled at me? Why are we talking about the nice woman instead of the man who told the pit bull to attack me?"

The detective hit Play and said, "Keep watching."

The police officers finally moved enough so that the person in the wheelchair was visible. It was a man. He looked withered and old. He had a beard, but the beard was snowy white.

A dog tottered down the ramp and sat beside the wheelchair. It was a spaniel of some type, not a pit bull. The spaniel leaned its head against the man's knee. They resembled two old friends sitting in a park.

Maribel whispered, "Oh, Sabina, how could you?"

Luke cleared his throat and looked away.

Sabina got to her feet and demanded, "Who else was in the van? That's not the man I saw. Did you look inside?"

The detective stopped the video. He closed the laptop, saying, "Those were the only passengers, Sabina. We opened every door and compartment. The gentleman asked his daughter to take him for a ride around Sanibel Island today before going back to the hospital."

"Hospital?" the girl asked softly.

"That's right. He's very ill. His daughter told me privately they don't expect him to live much longer. She thought this might be their last day together away from the hospital."

Maribel's eyes began to tear up when the detective explained, "They'd seen your picture, Sabina, and read the article. In his younger days he was a commercial fisherman. The gentleman was impressed. His daughter thought it might be fun for her dad to actually meet you. So they took a chance, and there you were, walking on the bike path."

Detective Miller put his computer away. "Now do you understand why I wanted to speak privately? Sabina, you made a mistake. It's up to you to admit it. The gentleman and his daughter will be satisfied with that. If you don't, there could be trouble."

The girl, with her stubborn jaw, thought about it for a long second. Finally she muttered, "Okay. I made a stupid mistake. There—I said it."

The detective appeared puzzled, then apparently decided

he didn't like her attitude. "One more thing—and please listen closely. No more calls about this shark fins nonsense. Making up stories is the wrong way to get your picture in the paper, young lady. Understand?"

"I understand," the girl said, staring straight ahead.

The detective was clearly frustrated. "You know what the worst thing is? There really is a gang of poachers out there. They don't fish during the day—our boats would have spotted them. They don't seem to fish at night, either—we have helicopters with night-vision electronics. So the mystery is, what time of day or night can poachers net sharks without being seen? Maybe that fifty-thousand-dollar reward will help produce a legitimate tip."

He sighed and looked at his watch. "We had a conference call meeting scheduled for this morning—crime experts from all over the country to help us solve that mystery. But guess what? Instead, we wasted our time looking for your black van, Sabina—and an old man in a wheelchair."

Detective Miller stood up. "Goodbye," he said to the trio. "I don't expect to see you three kids again. Understood?"

When the man was gone, Maribel glared at her sister.

Her eyes were red from crying. The two girls squabbled back in forth in Spanish until Luke intervened. "Instead of arguing, I'd rather get out on the water. Think about it. This might be the last time we're allowed to use the boat. So we might as well fish while we can."

"It's too late in the afternoon," Maribel said while her sister scowled and toyed with her necklace. "Besides, Hannah didn't say we could fish."

"She didn't say we couldn't," Luke countered.

The boy's brazen attitude surprised both of the Estéban sisters. Sabina was impressed. "I agree with the farm boy. I vote we go shark tagging." She raised her hand and stared until Luke raised his.

Maribel, still angry, was reluctant but slowly raised her hand. "Okay. It's unanimous, I guess. I'll go get the boat ready. But we have to go soon because we have to be back before sunset. So be ready to leave in ten minutes."

When she was gone, Sabina said to Luke, "She's still mad. Why aren't you mad at me?"

"Waste of time," the boy grumbled. "I've got to grab some frozen chum."

"Wait—I wasn't lying," she said. "The old man in the video wasn't the man I saw in the back of that van. I don't care what anyone says—it was the drunkard who ordered his dog to attack me. The dog, too. I recognized its growl. It's that woman who's lying. The man I saw must have gotten out, and she kept driving."

Once again, the girl was surprised when Luke replied, "I know. The guy in the wheelchair must be part of their gang, too."

"*What?* You actually believe me?"

"Of course I do," Luke said. "There were two men in the back of the van when the woman asked you to sign the newspaper. What's so hard to believe about that? One got out before the police stopped her. The pit bull probably went with him."

Sabina, who didn't like hugging anyone, suddenly wanted to hug this strange boy, despite the stupid gloves on his hands. "That makes me feel better, so I take back all the mean things I've said about you. Everybody else in the world thinks I'm a crazy liar."

"Maybe," the boy responded, "but you're not a liar." He said this with a rare half smile.

The girl was still thinking about that while she packed their lunch for fishing. Had he made a joke at her expense? Why else the sly smile?

They were in the boat, Maribel at the controls, and heading for Fools Cut when Sabina finally figured out his sly joke.

"Hey, farm boy," she snapped. "I'm not crazy, either!"

It was midafternoon when they anchored in Fools Cut. Soon they would catch the largest and strangest-looking fish they had ever seen. But it would take a while.

First they had to get set up. There was a lot to do before they could actually start fishing. Luke lowered the chum bag over the side. He helped Sabina rig two rods, and she casted the baits out. They secured the rods in their holders and did what all anglers do—sat and waited.

It became obvious to Luke that the sisters weren't speaking to each other.

Good, he thought at first. Sometimes they made his ears tired the way they chattered back and forth. But he knew they couldn't go on this way as a team.

What could he do to smooth things over?

Luke had spent his life avoiding conversations. He'd

rarely been in a situation that required him to actually *start* one.

So he waited for his chance to get the girls talking.

It was hot. The afternoon breeze wilted into stillness beneath the Florida sun. Occasionally a gust stirred a musky odor from the mangroves. It was a sulfur smell, like boiled eggs. Trees crowded in on both sides of the boat.

Fools Cut was narrow.

Mosquitoes spun silver clouds in the shade. Some insects ventured out into the sunlight. The boy swatted a big one, full of blood, on his arm.

This provided a reason to say to Sabina, "Would you mind asking your sister for the bug spray?"

"Ask her yourself," the girl replied.

He tried again by addressing both girls. "Are mosquitoes this bad in Cuba? Someone told me that only female mosquitoes bite. Is that true?"

Sabina grumbled, "Probably because the males are too lazy to find food."

Maribel wanted to make peace, so she risked saying, "Only the females bite because they have to drink blood before laying their eggs. We studied that in science in fifth grade. The blood can be from a deer or a rabbit or a person. Any mammal. They need it for energy."

Luke sensed an opening. "You're going into fifth grade, aren't you, Sabina?"

"Who cares," the girl responded, and used a stubborn chin to indicate her sister. "Ask her. She knows everything."

I give up, the boy thought.

But he couldn't give up. This might be the very last tagging trip for Sharks Incorporated, so it had to be a success. He had to think of a topic so interesting the sisters would forget they were angry. He stared at his hands. He focused on the bulky farmer's gloves that covered them.

Suddenly, Luke knew a way.

But was it worth sharing his secret?

This required some thought.

If he revealed the burn scar, there was a risk that kids at school would find out. He would be taunted, possibly. Bullied, maybe, by the older kids because the lightning scars set him apart as different from everyone else. And on the baseball field, yeah, there was no doubt he'd be made fun of. Baseball players loved assigning nicknames for oddball reasons.

For instance, the guys on his Little League team in Ohio (the Pioneer Eagles) had called Luke "Hay Hook." Hay hooks were large, sharp hooks used to snatch bales of hay or straw onto a wagon. One hot afternoon, Luke had swung at a bale of hay but missed and had buried the hook into his leg. The result was a scar on his shin that was barely noticeable.

As nicknames went, Hay Hook wasn't bad. In fact, it was sort of cool. But what would guys in the dugout call a kid with two lightning scars that were as weird as circus tattoos?

No, too risky, he decided.

He argued the subject back and forth in his head. Should he take off his gloves and share the truth. Or leave them on?

Share.

The word caused him to remember something. It had to do with the bittersweet smile on his aunt's face that morning in the lab. There was a sadness he didn't understand when she'd said, *New friends aren't nearly as important as old friends you can share your secrets with.*

He hadn't understood Hannah's sadness. But he finally had to admit the sisters were his friends. This wasn't easy to admit, even to himself, because they were girls—but so what? They were also his teammates. And teammates share.

Luke stood suddenly and announced, "Hey, you two, stop acting like kids. I want to show you something."

Maribel paid attention when the boy took off his left glove and placed it on the console.

Sabina's eyes widened as he removed his right glove. She started to say, "If you want me to read your palm, we should—"

That's as far as she got.

The scream of a fishing reel interrupted her.

"Fish on!" Maribel yelled.

They all rushed to do their jobs.

SEVENTEEN
A RAY, A DINOSAUR,
AND A SEA COW

It wasn't a shark that took the bait. It was a stingray—the first they'd ever caught.

It was Maribel's turn to take the rod, but she delegated the job to Sabina, hoping to end their feud.

Her kindness seemed to help. When the younger sister saw what was on the end of her line, she hollered, "Maribel, stay back, it's a stingray! Look at how long its tail is. Luke, put your stupid gloves on, and keep away from that stinger."

The ray was the size of a doormat. Wide, rounded wings slapped the water when it came to the surface. Its tail was a yard long. The barb on the end smacked the side of the boat like a bullwhip.

"It looks like Batman's flying car," Sabina whooped.

Luke, who loved Batman, agreed. The ray was flat bodied and sleek, blackish brown on top. Its eyes were set deep in what resembled a space vehicle designed to cruise among the stars.

He was relieved to have his gloves on again. The sisters appeared to be getting along just fine.

Maribel shot video. Luke used a paddle to control the ray's tail, and a long-handled hook remover to free the creature.

The stingray righted itself, flapped its wings, and flew away like an underwater bird.

Seconds later the second fishing rod buckled. Another big fish caused the reel to clatter.

It was Luke's turn on the rod, but he said, "Maribel, you take it."

The older sister replied, "No, it's all yours." Good captains, she was learning, put the happiness of their crew ahead of their own.

The boy didn't argue. He wrestled the rod from its holder and held on. "It's a big one," he said. "Look at it go."

Line peeled off the reel as the fish ran. The line ripped a crevice across the water fifty yards behind the boat and kept going.

The sisters weren't sure it was a shark, but they got the tagging equipment ready, anyway. This included the polished new amber pole that Luke had made.

"I don't think it's a blacktip," the boy said after a few minutes. "It hasn't jumped."

There was another difference he noticed. Small sharks raced away like rockets. This fish pulled with the steady force of a tractor. The boy had the rod anchored against his belly. He used both hands to leverage the rod up. Whenever he got a chance, he cranked the reel to recover a few feet of line.

Just as fast, whatever had taken the bait powered its way farther and farther from the boat.

Twenty minutes went by. "It's too big," Maribel decided. "We've got to let it go."

"Not yet!" Sabina protested.

"I don't want to, either," the older sister said. "But those are the rules."

Maribel was worried about something else. In June, it rained almost every afternoon, and it was getting late. She had yet to hear thunder, but in the far distance there were mountainous black clouds.

The boy was sweating, still battling the fish.

"Did you hear me, Luke? We don't have a choice. You know what Dr. Ford said to do if a fish is too big to handle."

They were using special fishhooks designed to bend free before the line broke.

"Tighten the drag," she instructed, "so the fish can bend the hook and get away."

Luke hesitated, then conceded, "Yeah, darn it. You're right. But I sure would like to see what it is."

Maribel was relieved. Hannah had told her that good captains never have to raise their voices or say, "That's an order."

There was a knob on the front of Luke's spinning reel. It could be adjusted so that it was impossible to pull line off the spool. She watched the boy screw the knob down tight and brace himself.

Luke felt the rod bend with such force that it threatened to pull him off the boat. Then suddenly the rod sprang back and the line went slack.

"Lost it," he said, cranking in line. "Doggone it. I bet it was another big bull shark, you think?" An instant later, it was no longer easy to turn the reel. "Hey . . . ," he said. "Hey! The fish is still hooked, and it's coming straight toward the boat."

Sabina hooted and got the new tagging pole ready. Luke lifted hard . . . lowered the rod quickly and reeled. Over and over, he repeated the procedure until the fish was beneath the boat. With a final effort, he lifted and they all looked down.

Maribel gasped. "Oh my goodness . . . it looks like a dinosaur."

"What is it?" Sabina asked. "Should we tag it?"

"I'm not sure," Luke said.

They had never seen anything like the fish at the end of the line. Its body was six feet long, with wide fins like wings. It looked a little bit like a shark. But it sort of looked like a stingray, too—except for one obvious difference: Protruding from the fish's nose was a long toothy blade. The blade resembled a sword edged with teeth.

"Get the book," he suggested. "I think it's a sawfish. They're really rare." The fish had stopped struggling. Using the slow sweep of its tail against the current, the creature seemed content to rest peacefully on the surface beside the boat.

There was a locker beneath the boat's steering wheel. Maribel retrieved a book titled *Marine Fishes of Florida*. She flipped through the pages but was interrupted by an ominous rumble. It was followed by a sharp blast of thunder.

"We don't have time to look it up," she said, glancing skyward. "There's a storm coming. We've got to get back to the marina."

"Should I tag it?" Sabina asked again. She couldn't take her eyes off the strange fish. It was longer than she was tall and had rough cinnamon-colored skin. The girl was eager to be the first to try the new tagging pole.

"Whatever we do, let's do it quick," Luke said. "This fish is tired of being hooked. And I'm getting a little tired myself. It's gotta weigh close to a hundred pounds."

Maribel considered the towering clouds over the mainland. They had yet to feel a chilly blast of wind that would signal the storm was moving their way. That suggested it would be a while before they were in danger of being drenched or struck by lightning.

"Give me a second." She had found the book's index. "Here it is," she said. "Yes, it's a sawfish—a small-tooth sawfish."

"Small?" Sabina said. "That thing is huge. I think we should tag it before it gets mad."

Maribel read from the book: "'Sawfish look somewhat like sharks, but with their wide fins and flatter bodies, they are really an ancient relative of stingrays. Their nose, instead of teeth, has a specialized sword that resembles a saw. They use this saw to stun small fish before eating them. Sawfish grow to over eighteen feet long.'"

Eighteen feet? They actually had caught a dinosaur—a young one!

Maribel skimmed ahead. "You're right, Luke. They're rare. Listen to this: 'Loss of habitat and overfishing have destroyed most of the sawfish population. In the United States, the last remaining population of sawfish live off south Florida.'"

"Then I am going to tag it," Sabina said. She leaned over the boat with the new tagging pole in both hands. "Scientists somewhere have to be studying sawfish."

Maribel nodded, convinced. "You're right. I'll get the camera."

We really are good at what we do, Luke thought. They had tagged, measured, and estimated the sawfish's weight in less than three minutes. It gave him a good feeling to watch the big fish swim away unhurt. He was also pleased the tagging pole had worked perfectly.

The sisters congratulated each other on another good job. Luke shared some fist bumps, then went to the front of the boat to pull the anchor. The storm was still miles away, but it was coming. As he reached for the rope, a dark shape in the water caught his attention. For an instant, he froze, then began to back away.

Maribel noticed. "What's wrong?"

The boy didn't respond. Something gigantic was swimming toward their boat. The animal—whatever it was—was the size of a bear, and as hairless as the prize pigs he'd raised in 4-H.

Luke stood and watched, mystified.

The animal surfaced for an instant . . . went under, then continued toward them. Its progress beneath the water could be followed by watching shiny swirls on the surface.

"What's wrong?" Maribel asked again. She was frightened by the look on Luke's face.

Finally he whispered, "Did you see that?"

Sabina said, "Of course not. You see everything before we do—and it's not fair." She moved beside him. "Where? I don't see anything."

"Hang on to your seats," Luke warned. "It's going to ram our boat any second now."

"Ram us?"

"Yeah—grab something!"

He watched the animal's wake spin circles on the surface. The creature arrowed closer and closer . . . then vanished beneath the boat.

After several tense seconds waiting for an impact, the boy muttered, "Where the heck did it go?"

"Is this a joke?" Sabina demanded. "I was just starting to like you a little bit."

"I don't see anything, either," Maribel said. "Is it a shark— or a bigger sawfish?"

Cautiously, Luke leaned over the side. Beneath them was a massive shadow. The shape was oddly familiar. But he couldn't admit that what he saw resembled a giant swimming pig. The pig—or whatever it was—had a big, broad tail shaped like a shovel.

"It looks like, I don't know . . . a small whale, maybe," he stammered.

"A whale," Sabina said. "And people say I'm crazy. Water in this bay isn't deep enough for whales."

That was true. "What it really looks like," Luke said, "is a . . . well, a giant pig with a big flipper for a tail."

The younger girl thought his words were hilarious. "Pig farmer, that's what I'll call you from now on."

He ignored her laughter and watched the shadow float upward. When the deck jolted beneath their feet, Sabina went rigid. Her face paled. The boat jolted again and began to rock.

"What's happening?" she yelled.

Until then Maribel had been frightened, too. Not now, because she had experienced something similar one day out in Captain Hannah's boat. "There's nothing to be afraid of," she said. "Keep watching. You'll understand what I mean."

In Spanish, Sabina said, "Is everyone crazy? There's nothing funny about a giant pig attacking our boat. Do something!"

Luke wasn't convinced, either. When the snout of a large animal spouted water beside the boat, he jumped back, saying, "There it is!"

The animal was huge—the size of two pigs in one body that was gray-black and splotched with barnacles.

"Don't worry, it's harmless," Maribel said with a laugh. "It's a manatee. They're like giant teddy bears that eat grass and sea squirts and things. They're vegetarians that wouldn't harm a fly."

"Man-a-tee?" Luke repeated so he would remember the name.

"Some people call them sea cows," Maribel explained. "They like to scratch their backs on boats and pilings and stuff. Sabina, you've seen manatees around the marina. Why were you so afraid?"

"I wasn't afraid," the girl insisted. "Well . . . not until the pig farmer here told me our boat was about to be rammed." She knelt for a closer look at the manatee. "Awww," she cooed. "See how cute its face is? Luke, what's wrong with you? In Ohio, does everything resemble a pig?"

The animal lounged on the surface for a while. It spouted and snorted as if enjoying the attention. When it nosed toward the bottom, a huge fluke tail appeared and slapped the water.

At the same instant, a thunderous boom echoed through the mangroves. A fresh gust of wind chilled the late-afternoon air. They still had an hour or so of daylight left, but they couldn't risk getting caught in a thunderstorm.

"We've got to get moving," Maribel said. "Luke, pull the anchor. Sabina, would you mind putting the rods away?"

The younger sister had been startled by the nearby lightning strike. She obeyed instantly, saying, "No kidding, we've got to go."

Overhead, the sky had grayed. Clouds were laced with eerie green light.

Luke should have been the first to notice the color of the sky. He didn't. "Hold on . . . Something's wrong," he said from the front of the boat.

"Now what?" Sabina groaned.

Usually their anchor was marked by a Styrofoam ball attached to the anchor line, as a safety precaution. If they had to abandon the anchor for some reason, it could be found later because the ball floated. But the Styrofoam ball was gone.

"We're drifting," he said. "Feel it? The boat's swinging, and our anchor's missing."

Maribel had already noticed. The tide was carrying them through Fools Cut toward open water outside the bay. And leaving the bay was forbidden.

She started the engine. "Everyone, stop what you're doing and sit down," she said. But when she tried to turn, the boat would not turn. She pushed the throttle forward. The engine strained as if the boat had snagged something heavy beneath the water.

It had snagged something. Luke figured it out. "The manatee got tangled in our anchor line. Look!"

Thirty feet in front of the boat, the animal surfaced. Looped around its tail was a jumble of rope and the Styrofoam ball.

"We're not drifting," he said. "The manatee's pulling us. We've got to cut the anchor line, or it's going to pull us out of Dinkins Bay."

Cutting the anchor line seemed like a good idea until Sabina cried, "Wait—we can't! The poor thing will die trying to drag all that rope and our anchor. We've got to untangle it. See—it's already getting tired."

The manatee was on its side, slapping its tail. Battling against the weight of the boat had exhausted the creature.

Maribel remained calm and tried to think. The wind had picked up. The air was cold, fragrant with the scent of rain. The animal had pulled them through the cut. Ahead lay a space of green water and waves, where a silent thread of lightning flickered in the distance, then vanished.

Seconds later—*Boommmmm!*—rolling thunder vibrated in their ears.

Luke winced. "Maribel," he said, "let's get the heck out of here. I don't want to get struck by lightning again. Trust me, *it hurts*."

Both girls stared at him.

"*Again?*" they asked in unison.

The boy stammered, "Uh, well, yeah—almost a month ago. I was going to tell you, but—"

Another bolt of lightning brightened the sky. Thunder hammered at their ears.

Maribel looked at the struggling animal, then at Luke and her younger sister. "We can't talk about this now. If we work fast, we might be able to cut the manatee free before the storm gets here. It's up to you both. If I have to make the choice, our safety comes first. Everyone, double-check the snaps on your life jackets!"

As they adjusted their inflatable suspenders, a blast of wind spun through the mangroves. Sabina raised her voice to ask Luke, "What's it like to be struck by lightning? I *hate* lightning. Why aren't you dead?"

The boy cleared his throat and swallowed. The stormy hues of the sky—neon green and pinkish purple—mimicked the colors throbbing in his head. For some reason, those familiar colors calmed him.

"The doctor said maybe I was for a few seconds," Luke replied.

He turned to Maribel. "Lightning really sucks. It's like your body's on fire—that's the way I felt. So if we're going to cut that thing loose, let's hurry up. It'll suck even worse if we're not back to the marina by sundown."

EIGHTEEN
A FREE MANATEE AND A MYSTERY SOLVED

Water on both sides of the boat was shallow. Small waves were beginning to whitecap along a sandbar on the outside fringe of Dinkins Bay. Maribel remembered the detective mentioning the sandbar. He'd said that, aside from Fools Cut, there was no deep water. No boat larger than a canoe could anchor on this side of the mangroves.

The manatee seemed to know exactly where it was going. It dragged their boat and anchor through a narrow, twisting channel toward a vast area of open gray water.

Maribel, at the steering wheel with the engine running, followed at a slightly faster speed. As they drew closer to the manatee, Sabina coiled the anchor line. Luke stood nearby with a knife, ready in case she got tangled.

"One of us will have to get in the water when we're close enough," he called to Maribel. "I've caught lots of calves and stuff that got loose from their pens. I'm willing to go over the side and untangle the anchor if you want. Just tell me when."

In Spanish, Sabina said to her sister, "Is there any animal the pig farmer hasn't caught and eaten?"

Maribel was focused on keeping the boat and her passengers safe. "Luke, get the spare anchor ready. Sabina, you'll drop the anchor when I tell you. Luke and I will go over the side. And, everyone—tighten the straps on your life vests."

The boy did as he'd been told. The spare anchor was in a forward hatch. It wasn't as heavy as the one the manatee was dragging. Hopefully, it would be enough to prevent the boat from drifting away when he and Maribel went over the side.

"Do you want the anchor tied to the front of the boat or off the stern?" he yelled over the noise of the wind.

Stern was another word for the rear area of a vessel.

Maribel had been wondering the same thing. The anchor was more likely to dig into the bottom and hold if dropped off the front of the boat. But the channel was so narrow, she doubted there was room to turn the boat around if there was any emergency.

"The stern, I guess," she hollered.

The boy brushed past her. He tied the coil of rope attached to the extra anchor on a cleat near the engine, then hurried forward to get ready to jump over the side.

The manatee was only a few yards ahead of them now. Luke looked down and saw white half-moon scars on the animal's back, which meant a boat's propeller had hit the slow-moving creature before. Patches of barnacles dappled its grayish skin. The texture reminded him of elephants he'd seen at the Toledo Zoo.

"Do sea cows bite?" he asked Sabina. The girl was beside him on her knees.

"Probably—if you look like a vegetable," she reasoned. "Let me know if it hurts."

"Thanks," the boy responded. "I will."

Thunder rumbled in the gusting wind. Webs of lightning flared above a distant island.

Behind them Maribel called, "Sabina, get ready to drop the anchor. Luke, when we're close enough, wave or something and I'll shift the engine into neutral. I don't want to hit the poor thing."

The younger sister hurried to the back of the boat. Luke tightened his gloves and retied his Michael Jordan basketball shoes. His heart was banging against his ribs, yet he felt okay. He might not be good at starting a conversation between two angry sisters, but wrestling animals to the ground was something he *was* good at.

Trouble was, this was the ocean, not a barnyard. And the animal he was about to wrestle weighed as much as a small cow.

The manatee sensed the boat closing in from above. With a flick of its tail, it veered onto a sandbar so shallow that its whole body was soon exposed.

Luke signaled by waving his hand.

"*Now,*" Maribel ordered. "Sabina, drop the anchor."

The girl did. "Ready!" she called.

Maribel shifted the engine into neutral and rushed to join Luke near the bow, or the front of the boat.

"Let's make this quick—" she started to say, but the boy was already over the side. She watched him stumble, fall, then stumble and nearly fall again before standing up in knee-deep water.

"Come on," he hollered. "Wait—" He turned with an outstretched hand. "Give me the knife."

She did. It was a fishing knife with a red plastic handle.

The manatee was on its side, struggling to return to deeper water. Luke sensed the animal's terror. He approached slowly. He made soft clucking sounds as if calming a nervous horse.

The whole time, he stared and tried to communicate with the manatee as he often did with Pete, the retriever, and other dogs he'd trained. *You're safe . . . you're safe*, he told the animal silently. *I won't hurt you.*

When he was close enough, he dropped to his knees in the water. Then slowly he reached and stroked the manatee's back. The skin was rough and rubbery.

The animal snorted and seemed to sigh. Its breath smelled of mud and cut weeds.

Maribel sloshed up from behind. "Keep rubbing its back," she whispered. "It seems to like that. Give me the knife and I'll cut the rope."

What the manatee liked better, Luke discovered, was to have its back scratched hard. The harder the better. So he scratched and scratched and thought calming thoughts until Sabina hollered from the boat, "Hey! The anchor's not holding."

Maribel had cut the last tangle from the animal's tail.

When she turned, she saw their boat—and her sister—drifting away. Without thinking, she tossed the rope aside, and ran.

That was a mistake the young captain would soon regret.

Luke and Maribel charged after the boat until the boy realized they'd left the manatee stuck on the sandbar. "Keep going," he hollered, then turned and slogged back. He made the familiar clucking sounds and stood over the creature. *I'm going to help you*, he said without speaking.

The manatee belched air in response. Five hundred pounds of muscle and blubber was struggling to squirm into deeper water. Tiny arms that resembled fins clawed at the sand. The animal's huge fluke tail banged away but didn't make much progress.

Don't bite me, Luke thought.

He knelt, got his arms around the animal's neck, and used his legs to lift. It took every ounce of strength to pivot the thing a few feet closer to the channel.

Twice more he did it. When he sensed the manatee was about to panic, he used a trick he'd learned to calm frightened horses. After removing his inflatable vest straps, he took off his shirt and tied it around the animal's big, blunt head like a blindfold.

Again he knelt . . . lifted . . . took a few tiny steps, then lowered the massive head to the sand. Over and over he did this. The process was exhausting.

Maribel's voice reached the boy over the sound of wind and the thudding of his own heart. "Luke, come on. I need your help!"

She was in water up to her waist. Storm clouds floated toward the trio from the east. Wind pushed their drifting boat faster than Maribel could run or swim. Sabina, at the steering wheel, couldn't get the engine started.

The boy gave a last mighty effort. The manatee snorted and wallowed itself closer to the channel, where there was enough water to use its tail.

"Hang on a second," he yelled—not to Maribel, but to the manatee. He managed to snatch his shirt away just before the animal swam off.

Sabina got lucky, too. A plume of exhaust told him the engine was running. The younger sister clunked the throttle forward and steered toward Maribel. Soon both girls were in the boat, sopping wet but safe. Next Luke hefted himself over the side. He was bare chested and carried his shirt balled up in a gloved hand.

"You're incredible," Maribel told her sister, and gave her a hug. She couldn't help laughing with relief. "Did you pull up the spare anchor?"

Sabina replied, "Yes, but I don't know why. I hate that anchor. All it does is drag the bottom. Let's get out of here. It'll be dark soon, and that storm's coming. We've got to hurry."

The girl was right. A wall of rain drifted toward them. It was a sodden gray like smoke. The storm was still a few miles away, but bolts of wild electricity sometimes reached ahead of the clouds and zapped the water.

Maribel attempted to reward her sister by asking, "Do you want to drive us back to the marina? You've done a good job so far."

No, Sabina was happy to step away from the controls. While her sister steered them expertly into the narrow channel, the girl plopped down in the front seat next to Luke. "I can't believe you moved that manatee all by yourself," she said—then her gaze landed on the boy's bare shoulder. Her eyes widened when she saw the strange design that was burned into his skin.

"What . . . ? Where did you get that?" she stammered.

Luke rushed to put his wet shirt on while the girl continued to stare. "Maribel," she hollered. "You've got to see this."

"Not now," the older sister said. She was struggling to keep the boat in the channel.

"You've got to. Look at Luke's shoulder. It's the most beautiful tattoo I've ever seen. Farm boy"—she tugged at Luke's shirt sleeve—"take that off and show her. How much did it cost? I want a tattoo just like that when I can afford it."

Luke yanked away with his arms folded.

If Maribel had not been distracted, she would have seen the Styrofoam buoy ahead. It floated in the middle of the channel, still attached to the rope and anchor she'd recently tossed aside.

The boat lurched when it hit the buoy. It lurched again when the propeller snagged the rope. The engine struggled briefly, then quit with a harsh metallic *thunk*.

"Drop the spare anchor," Maribel ordered. She hurried to the back of the boat and tilted the motor from the water, as they'd been taught.

Knotted around the propeller was a ball of twisted rope, the anchor and Styrofoam ball still attached.

"What a mess," she said. "We're going to have to cut this off."

The wind began to whistle through the mangroves. A veil of black rain pushed closer, beneath clouds where lightning sizzled.

Luke took one look at the propeller and knew the trio was in trouble. He dropped the spare anchor, allowed all the rope to play out, and tied it to a cleat. Soon he realized they were in bigger trouble than he'd thought. Sabina had been right about the spare anchor. It only slowed the boat as it dragged across the bottom. That's all. It wasn't heavy enough to hold them against a storm that roared across the water like a freight train.

"We'll have to use the oars," Maribel yelled.

The oars were heavy, each eight feet long and made of wood. Luke helped her fit them into the oarlocks. They sat side by side, just as they had practiced. "Stroke . . . stroke . . . stroke," the older sister called in rhythm.

It had been a calm day when they'd learned how to row in unison. What was easy then seemed impossible now because of the wild waves. Finally, they gave up and stored the oars. It was better to call the marina for help, Maribel decided. They would have to drift and hope for the best until the storm passed.

She found the handheld radio, put it to her lips, and pressed the Transmit key. Over and over she said, "Calling Dinkins Bay Marina, please come in." But the wind was so loud, the only response was static. If someone from the marina had replied, none of them heard it.

By then the storm was on them. What light and warmth remained in the setting sun was swallowed up by an icy, slow-moving darkness. Maribel sat close to Sabina. "Stay down and hold on," she whispered.

There was nothing else they could do.

The first raindrops hammered the boat with pellets that stung like ice. Clouds covered the sun, and the cascade began. It was like being trapped under a waterfall. Maribel felt her sister's small hand on her arm. Soon they were so cold that they used spare life jackets as pillows on the deck of the boat, out of the wind. The sisters huddled together for warmth.

"Luke," Maribel hollered. "Where are you?"

A silent blast of lightning showed her. The boy sat alone near the engine, his head up, eyes open. He seemed to be watching something.

"Do you see that?" he replied. "Over there. It's some kind of boat."

Thunder vibrated through the deck and found their bones. It made a response impossible.

Luke continued to focus on the boat skimming toward them along the shallow mangroves.

How could that be? he wondered. There were sandbars there that only a canoe could cross, according to the detective. But this was like no boat he'd ever seen. Its hull was as flat as a Frisbee. It was powered by a giant fan on the back.

The roar of the boat's engine blended with rumbling thunder.

The boat angled toward what looked like a much larger boat visible in the distance. A triad of lightning bolts revealed that the smaller boat was heading for a commercial-sized fishing trawler a mile or two away. Perhaps they were meeting for some reason.

But what was a fishing trawler—or any other boat—doing out in this storm?

Luke's mind went to work. He was trying to piece the puzzle together when the smaller, Frisbee-like vessel abruptly slowed. When it stopped and turned in their direction, the boy suspected the driver had seen them.

In his head, a familiar caution light flashed with sparks of red. But thoughts of danger were displaced by something Hannah had told him: Fishing trawlers used nets to drag the bottom—massive nets that sometimes required the help of a smaller vessel.

Nets . . . of course! Suddenly some of the pieces seemed to fit.

Detective Miller and other law enforcement people had been frustrated by their inability to capture—or even spot—the shark poachers at work. That mystery had caused the man to ask, "What time of day or night can poachers net sharks without being seen?"

The detective had said this as if there were no answer.

But there was an answer. And Luke had just figured it out.

"Someone's coming," he hollered to the girls.

The strange boat was speeding their way.

Despite the rain, Luke stared and focused, and saw what the girls did not. The driver of the boat was a big-shouldered man with a black beard. Sitting obediently at his side was the pit bull.

Now the boy was sure he had solved the mystery. The poachers fished only during lightning storms!

But why weren't they afraid of being struck dead?

That was a mystery he had yet to solve.

Storm clouds parted for an instant. A wall of rain magnified the size of a massive orange sun. The sun became a glowing cavern, low on the horizon. It glazed the water with smoky light. The glare blurred Sabina's vision. Raindrops pelted her face. It was impossible to see without shielding her eyes.

Yes! A boat was coming. She hoped it was driven by Captain Hannah. That made sense. The woman had come looking for them. Of course she would, because they weren't allowed to leave the bay, and fishing in a rainstorm was against the rules.

Also, Maribel had called for help on the handheld

radio. Maybe someone at the marina had heard despite all the static. Convinced, the girl lay back and pulled the towel over head.

Maribel was still shielding her eyes, straining to see. She knew that Hannah would be angry—until the woman understood the series of disasters that had caused the trio to break the rules.

As Hannah had warned them many times, "Bad things happen fast on the water."

It was a phrase the trio would remember the rest of their lives.

Maribel didn't suspect trouble until Luke came toward her, demanding, "Try the radio again! Call Mayday—maybe the Coast Guard will hear you. We've got to get away from that boat!"

That's when she noticed the boat's strange design. It was large and fast, and as flat as a saucer. It skimmed over shoals too shallow for a motor.

It was an *airboat*, she realized.

Airboats weren't common in the area. But she had seen several in the Everglades on their trips to Miami. Airboats were used to cross prairies of grass where there was little or no water. They were powered by an airplane propeller. The noise they made was deafening—yet not as loud as the thunderous squall that blazed around them.

You would need a canoe to anchor on that side of the mangroves, the detective had told them.

The detective was mistaken. Maybe he had never seen an airboat. This one was double the size of their rental boat and coming fast across a shoal where even a canoe couldn't go. Sitting next to the driver was a stocky-looking dog—a pit bull.

In that instant Maribel realized that her sister had been telling the truth about the shark fins she'd seen and the bearded man.

Sabina was still curled beneath a towel to keep off the stinging rain. The elder sister lifted the towel and said, "I'm sorry. I never should have doubted you."

"What did you do wrong this time?" Sabina snapped.

"You need to get up," Maribel responded. "A boat's coming."

The younger girl threw off the towel and struggled to keep her balance in the wild waves. Then she fell back when, nearby, a blinding light ignited a thunderous *boom* that rocked the water.

"That almost hit us!" the girl wailed. She pressed herself to the deck and reached for the towel. "Lightning's going to kill us all!"

Maribel feared it was true.

What she feared more, suddenly, was the approaching boat. The airboat had slowed. It was close enough that, even through a haze of rain, she could see the man at the controls. He sat atop a high tower. Water dripped from his long dark hair. Rain funneled off the point of his black beard.

Beside him a dog with a muscular head stood at attention. The way the animal danced, whining, suggested it was eager to leap onto their boat.

"Stay down!" Maribel commanded Sabina in Spanish. "If he sees you, he'll recognize you from the newspaper, and we're all in trouble."

The moment the words were out of her mouth, she knew it was the wrong thing to say.

Sabina hated taking orders. And her little sister wasn't afraid of anything.

Maribel felt helpless—until she remembered the little waterproof camera.

She reached for the camera, thinking, *Maybe the police will believe us this time.*

NINETEEN

THE POACHER'S THREAT AND LUKE'S PROMISE

Sabina wanted people to think she was fearless, even though it wasn't true. Like now. She was cold, wet, and huddled alone on a boat that was adrift in a storm. To her, the situation was scary, but she had experienced worse. She and Maribel had drifted for days, by themselves, on the Gulf Stream. Waves the size of buildings had swept them toward the unknown.

Twice rain squalls had brought lightning.

The memory of those nights in darkness still haunted the girl.

Lightning had no heart. In Cuba, after a hurricane, lightning had burned their house to the ground. It had scorched a neighbor's cow. Even magic chants with the aid of her necklace could not stop its mindless destruction.

Lightning had no soul.

Yet when she heard Maribel order her to "stay down . . . he'll see you!" the girl immediately sat up, then bounced to her feet.

"Why?" she demanded. "Who will see me?" Then asked, "And what is making that awful noise?"

It was a roaring sound similar to that of a small airplane.

Sabina shielded her eyes and spun around. She was startled by the sight of a boat speeding toward them. She grinned and waved her arms. "Over here!" she yelled through the rain.

Her grin melted when she saw the man who was driving. He sat atop a metal tower at the controls. On the deck below was the dog that had attacked her.

"Hide . . . please, he'll see you," Maribel pleaded. She grabbed her sister by the shoulders and tried to force her down.

Sabina wrestled away and faced the man when the boat pulled closer and stopped. "Stay away from us, you drunkard!" she screamed. "I'll tell the police and they'll arrest you. My friend the detective will put you in jail!"

The airboat's propeller was so loud that even Luke, standing on the stern, didn't hear all of the girl's threats. The bearded man couldn't hear, either. For sound protection he wore plastic earmuffs over a ball cap turned backward.

The man recognized Sabina. His look of surprise left no doubt when he spotted her from the tower. He snarled and pointed. Then his lips formed two soundless words: *It's you!*

Sabina clutched her beads and shook a small fist. "Leave us alone, you criminal—or you'll be sorry."

The man's head tilted back in laughter. The propeller kicked water into a froth as the airboat spun around so close it banged the side of the rental boat. He ripped the earmuffs off and killed the engine.

A sudden silence cloaked the sound of rain and thunder. The airboat and their little rental drifted side by side toward a jagged area of oysters and waves. To the west was a purple horizon. Beyond was the open sea.

"Well, well, well, look what I found," the man roared, looking down. "If it ain't the little girl with the big mouth. Get your picture in the newspaper lately?"

On the deck below the tower, the pit bull, barking, strained against a steel-studded leash.

"Shut up, dummy," the man commanded the dog.

The pit bull whimpered as if it had been whipped, and put its head down.

Luke frowned but said nothing. He sensed the animal's fear.

"When the police arrest you," Sabina shouted, "we'll be on television, too. And the internet! Now go away and leave us alone." She shook an angry fist—until she remembered they were in trouble. "Hey, mister?" she amended. "Before you go, would you mind lending us an anchor? My sister lost ours, and she broke our motor, too."

The man snorted through his beard and laughed. "From what I've heard, the police don't believe anything you brats say. In fact, I doubt they'd even bother to—" A thunderous bolt of lightning interrupted him. That's when he noticed Maribel doing something suspicious behind the steering wheel.

"Hey! What do you got there?" he yelled.

Maribel had the waterproof camera in video mode. Her hands shook as she positioned it atop the console. "Just our little radio," she lied. "I called for help, and they're on their way now."

"Liar," the man hollered. "No one can use their radio when I'm around"—he glanced at a strange-looking antenna behind his seat—"and I didn't hear no call for help to the Coast Guard."

"Not the Coast Guard, a friend of ours," Maribel answered. "She's a fishing guide at Dinkins Bay. We don't need any help. She and a bunch of other fishing guides will be here soon."

Sabina took this as the truth. It made her bolder. "I bet the police handcuff you and take you away in chains," she taunted. "Your mean dog, too. So give us your anchor and get out of here!"

The man thought that was hilarious. He scratched his jaw and looked north through the rain. Harsh sunlight showed a golden fringe of mangroves several miles away. A boat leaving Dinkins Bay would have to come from that direction. And there was no rescue boat to be seen.

Luke sensed the man thinking, *I've got plenty of time*.

The boy felt nervous and on edge, but not scared. The guy reminded him of his stepfather, the way he yelled orders. But Luke wasn't too nervous to memorize the airboat's registration number, which was printed plainly on the side. And he noticed a couple of oddities. On the boat's front deck was a mountain of heavy netting. It looked strong enough to entrap sharks. On the back of the boat, next to the propeller cage, was a small electric trolling motor—it could be used to move silently, unnoticed at night. Attached to the control tower was the strange-looking pole. It had to be twenty feet tall.

That's weird, he thought.

It wasn't a boat antenna. Marine antennas were fiberglass. This pole was metal, a couple of inches thick. It narrowed at the top, where there was a tiny cross bar wrapped with wire. So . . . maybe it was a different kind of antenna. But why leave it up during a thunderstorm?

Wondering about that, Luke drifted off into his own world for a moment. He returned when the man called to him, "Hey, you little twerp. I'm not gonna ask again! Are you gonna let these girls do your thinking for you, or toss me that rope? You're running out of time, bucko."

The boy realized he'd missed something important. "Sorry, mister," he called. "I didn't hear you."

"You heard just fine," the man shouted back. "I got work to do, sonny. I'll give you—" He lifted a thick arm to check his watch. "You got exactly one minute to make up your mind."

Luke moved closer to Maribel. "What's he talking about?"

"Don't do it," Sabina said. She had wiggled between them. "You didn't hear? He said he'll help get our motor started if I forget about seeing those shark fins. And we have to promise to never tell the police."

Maribel, with her sopping hair and T-shirt, did her best to stay calm. "We've got to do something. Look," she said, and pointed downwind to a shallow area. Waves hammered a long, jagged reef of oysters. "If we keep drifting, our boat will get beaten to pieces—and probably us, too. I don't trust that guy, but we need help. And we need it fast. Either that, or one of us has to get out and cut the rope off our propeller. The engine won't work unless we do."

"Hannah is on her way," the younger sister argued. "You said so yourself. I hope she brings Marion. Dr. Ford would tell that man to go straight to—"

"Quiet," Maribel said, and spoke to them both. "I lied about reaching Hannah. I don't know if she's coming. It's my decision, but, Luke, I want to know what you think."

Sabina bickered with her older sister while a nagging

detail surfaced in the boy's mind. He thought back to the laboratory, earlier in the day, when he'd said to his aunt, "I guess we won't be fishing for sharks today."

Guess not was Captain Hannah's reply.

So Hannah not only wasn't searching for them—she probably didn't know they'd gone out in the rental boat.

How could he have forgotten something so important?

A familiar tension knotted the boy's stomach. It was the same feeling he'd gotten back in Ohio when he'd lost his homework or the cool catcher's mitt he had worked so hard to buy. Two months of baling hay, the glove had cost him. Yet he'd left it in the dugout after a tournament in Bryan—a big town, by his standards.

And today, forgetting what Captain Hannah had said about not fishing was his biggest mistake by far.

From the tower of the airboat, the bearded man hollered, "You got thirty seconds, kiddies." He seemed to be having fun. He was trying to light a cigar, but the rain kept putting it out.

Luke pulled the girls closer until their faces nearly touched. "I did something stupid," he said. "I mean *really* stupid."

"What's new?" Sabina responded.

Maribel gave her sister a stern look. "Don't worry about that now. We all do stupid stuff."

"But you don't know what it is."

"Luke, we'll talk about it later. We have to make a decision"—she lifted her head and saw the oyster reef only a hundred yards away—"and we have to make it *now*. Can you cut that rope off the propeller? I have to be ready to start the engine if you can."

Maribel's kindness was like a reprieve. The boy stared at the pit bull for a moment, then studied the ball of rope knotted around the drive shaft. "Yep, I can do it," he said.

"Ten seconds," the man hollered. The cigar was lit, and he exhaled a cloud of smoke. "Don't be stupid, boy. Toss me that line before those oysters tear the bottom out of your boat."

Maribel whispered, "Are you sure, Luke? I don't want you to get hurt, and it's awful rough out here."

Luke saw confident shades of bluish silver in his mind. "Don't worry about it," he said, and thrust his jaw toward the bearded man. "Anything is better than trusting that big bucket load."

A moment later the man bellowed, "Time's up, kiddies. I'll warn you right now—if you talk to the cops or cross me again, I'll find you. I swear I will. And I'll beat your butts until they're raw. What do you have to say to that?"

On the deck below the tower, the pit bull gazed at Luke. It whined piteously and wagged its stubby tail.

Maribel was getting it all on camera. A flare of lightning showed her cheeks turning red. She stood and faced the shark poacher. Then she cupped her hands to her mouth to be heard. "Here's what we have to say to that," she said, and yelled a harsh-sounding phrase in Spanish. The girl whirled around as if she had better things to do.

The man responded with a few profane threats of his own and started his engine. The propeller kicked a jet stream of wind that caused the rental boat to spin like a leaf.

"Wait until I tell *mamá* what you said," Sabina hooted. By then the airboat was motoring away. "When she finds out, I'll be able to swear whenever I want."

The rain had slowed. The wind had picked up. Lightning bolts stabbed at the earth beneath an orange-sunset sky. Luke was retying his shoes, getting ready to go over the side again—until he saw the airboat accelerate and turn.

"He's coming back," he warned the sisters. "I don't like that guy. I think he's got a screw loose, and he'd kill us if he could."

TWENTY
ON THE RUN!

The rental boat was drifting toward disaster. Downwind, waves crashed over a jagged reef. From the opposite direction came the airboat at full speed. The man's wild long hair framed his eyes. His cigar was a spike that widened his grin.

"He won't hit us," Maribel insisted, yet sounded unsure. "He's a bully. But tighten your life vests just in case."

She and her sister had ducked behind the console for protection.

Luke knelt near the motor and adjusted the straps on an inflatable life vest that resembled a set of suspenders. A red string dangled from the left shoulder of the suspenders. Pull it, and the vest immediately inflated. The vest would also inflate if submerged in water—a safety precaution in case the wearer was unconscious and fell overboard.

Maribel put the handheld radio to her cheek. As the airboat neared, she pressed the Transmit button, and called, "Mayday, Mayday—we need help!" But she was again cut off by a terrible static noise.

Mayday, as they'd been taught, was an emergency code word that should have gotten an immediate response.

Maribel looked at Luke and shook her head. No one had heard the transmission. She had to wonder if the static had something to do with the airboat's strange antenna.

She tried again, saying, "Mayday, Mayday!" in a louder voice.

Her words were smothered by more static and the roar of the airboat speeding toward them.

"Grab something and hang on," she yelled, and braced herself for impact. But instead of ramming them, the airboat rocketed past so closely that the nose nearly clipped their broken motor. The gust from the propeller was almost worse than a collision. The wind stream sent bottles and the remains of their sack lunch flying. The blast was so intense that, for an instant, Sabina thought she would be blown out of the boat, too.

She nearly was.

On the console, the waterproof camera skittered toward the water. Maribel lunged and managed to grab the thing just in time.

The airboat turned. It circled updrift and pivoted so that the giant propeller was aimed at them. When the engine revved, a wall of wind hit the rental boat with the force of a tornado. The deck reared. The boat teetered wildly.

What's that man doing? The question was in Sabina's panicked reaction.

"He's trying to blow us onto the reef," Maribel shouted. "Get your shoes on—hurry, Sabina! We might be better off in the water."

A lightning bolt flashed nearby. Thunder muted the roar of the airboat briefly. It was almost impossible to be heard.

Luke had withdrawn into his own silent world. He focused on the bearded man. Only the guy's head was visible above the propeller cage unless the airboat swung to the right or left. Somehow the pit bull had climbed to the upper deck and was beside him.

No . . . Luke knew the truth. The man had dragged the dog up by its spiked collar. He was screaming at the animal for some reason. When the man raised a fist, the pit bull half jumped, half fell to the deck below.

Luke's jaw flexed. His eyes moved from the tangle of rope around their propeller to the heavy fishing rod he had used to land the sawfish. It was the same rod he had used at the marina to practice casting tennis balls for the retriever. And to improve the accuracy of his casting.

Next the boy's attention shifted to the airboat, with its massive propeller.

The bearded man was looking over his shoulder as if backing up a car. He yelled something—a threat, possibly. With the engine in neutral, he allowed the airboat to drift closer into what Luke, a baseball player, considered easy throwing distance. When the man hit the throttle again, the propeller's wind stream lifted their rental boat. A wall of air pushed it like a sled, faster and faster toward the jagged oysters.

"Inflate your life vests and get ready to jump!" Maribel called. She feared their boat would flip when it hit the reef. They might all be crushed.

Sabina glared at the man. She was chanting words she had learned at her favorite store in Havana.

Luke reached for the fishing rod. The special hook at the end of the line was designed to break easily. But the line was not. It was thick monofilament, strong enough to land a monster bull shark. Above the hook was a heavy lead sinker. When he freed the hook from an eyelet, the lead sinker swung like a miniature wrecking ball.

"Did you hear me, Luke?" Maribel demanded. "Inflate your life vest. We have to jump before we hit those oysters. They'll cut us to pieces."

The boy didn't have to look. He knew they had only a minute or two before their boat slammed onto the reef. He could hear waves breaking over the razor-sharp shells.

"Don't wait on me," he responded. "I'm coming." To convince the girl, he yanked the string on his life vest. With a *whoosh* the inflatable suspenders ballooned around his neck.

Sabina went over the side first. After a frightened glance at the boy, Maribel followed her sister.

Without hesitating, Luke raised the fishing rod in both hands. He leaned back for leverage. When he felt the rod bend, he took aim and catapulted the fishing line forward at the airboat. The lead sinker hit the propeller cage like a gunshot.

For a moment he thought the sinker had dropped

harmlessly into the water. But when the rod was nearly snatched from his hands, he knew the line had tangled in the huge wooden blade.

Fishing line streamed off the reel. The boy's arms weren't strong enough to hang on to the rod, so he dropped to the deck and braced his feet against the cooler. Slowly the rental boat turned. It was like a giant fish being dragged toward the spinning propeller.

The bearded man, wearing earmuffs, didn't notice. He looked over his shoulder again and grinned at the sight of the two sisters floundering in the waves. To him, this was proof that the kids who had pestered him were in serious trouble. If they survived crashing onto the reef, that was okay, too.

"The police don't believe anything you brats say," he taunted.

When the poacher was satisfied with what he'd done, he shouted something that sounded final and dismissive. He turned and didn't look back. His attention was on the fishing trawler anchored in the distance through the rain.

Luke clung to the rod as the airboat idled away. It began to tow the rental boat but at a much slower speed than the line melting off the reel. Their fishing reels, Hannah had told them, held nearly a quarter mile of stout monofilament. The boy knew that soon every inch of his line would be wrapped around the airboat's propeller. But unlike the rope that had disabled their boat, the fishing line seemed to have no effect on the much larger engine.

In a way, he was relieved. He'd lost his temper, which was dumb to begin with. And what if the airboat had been disabled? They would've all been stuck on the same reef with an angry, big-shouldered man who'd cut the fins off sharks while they were still alive—and who'd left Luke and the sisters to be cut to pieces by oyster shells.

The airboat slowed for a moment. The bearded man was talking to someone on a VHF radio. It gave the boy a chance to get a better grip on the fishing rod and glance at the reel.

The spool was nearly empty.

For the first time he heard the sisters calling to him. Their words were swept away by rain and thunder. But they appeared to be okay as they bobbed toward a sandy area where waves crashed but there were no oysters.

Luke had to decide: Should he hang on to the rod until the line broke? If he did, the rental boat might be towed a safe distance away from the oyster reef. He'd be able to hop overboard and cut the rope off their propeller.

But what if the fishing line didn't break?

What if the airboat suddenly accelerated?

It *happened*.

The bearded man, done talking on the radio, slammed the throttle forward. The airboat reared like a horse, then rocketed off.

Luke braced himself as the last of his fishing line peeled away. When there was no more line, the impact was worse than he could have imagined. Instead of breaking, the reel shattered because the line was knotted to the spool. He was nearly dragged overboard. He battled to hang on, but the rod was wrenched from his hands. It flew skittering across the water as if in pursuit of the airboat's propeller.

The boy got up and cupped his hands around his eyes. By then the airboat was a football field away. Even he couldn't see exactly what happened when the fishing rod hit the propeller cage. But he heard a ratcheting *BANG*. Next came the screech of metal on metal. The massive engine revved out of control for several seconds. The airboat zigzagged in a wild circle, and then there was another, much louder metallic *BOOM*.

Something inside the engine had exploded.

Luke, the novice mechanic, thought, *It blew a cylinder head*.

Maybe so, because the airboat was suddenly and silently adrift.

It was a few minutes before sunset. In the dusky-bronze light, the bearded man appeared in silhouette. He stood and looked back. Distance shrunk his size and the width of his shoulders. But his bearish voice carried across the water.

"You'll pay for this, you brats!" he bellowed. "Stay where you are—I'm coming. And if you run, by God, I'll find you."

Hearing that was scary enough. Even scarier was when the airboat turned and began to glide slowly, silently toward them.

How was that possible?

An electric trolling motor, Luke realized. He remembered seeing it mounted next to the propeller cage.

The boy grabbed an oar and paddled their rental boat toward the sandbar where the sisters stood among a jumble of waves. But the wind was too strong. It continued to push the boat toward the oysters.

Finally he gave up and slipped over the side into water up to his hips, sometimes his shoulders. It varied with the height of the waves. With him he took a rope attached to the front of the boat. He used it as a tow line. The inflatable suspenders dug at his neck when every fourth or fifth wave caught him from the side. Staying on his feet wasn't easy. He slogged and bounced and swam the boat toward the sandbar. When he was close enough, he hollered, "The guy's after us. We've got to get our propeller untangled."

The sisters had waded out to meet him.

"What happened?" Maribel called. "Did his engine quit?"

Beside her, Sabina clutched her necklace. "That'll teach that drunkard to mess with me," she said with a wicked grin. Then grimaced at the sound of a nearby lightning strike.

Luke realized the sisters hadn't seen what he'd done with the fishing rod—and it didn't matter. "We've got to hurry. If you two can hold the boat steady, I'll get the knife and start cutting that rope."

"There might be a safer way," Maribel said. She motioned for the boy to follow. "Come on."

"How? He'll catch us. He has an electric motor on that thing."

The older girl pointed to an opening in the mangroves. "Not if we hide. Maybe he'll give up after a while."

"But we can't get our boat across that sandbar," Luke argued.

"If Maribel says we can, we *can*," Sabina shot back. "If you haven't figured out how to do it, the drunkard probably can't, either. Hurry up and do as my sister says."

Together, the trio pulled the rental boat as far as they could onto the sandbar. Small cresting waves hammered at the back of the boat. Then a series of much larger waves lifted the hull and floated it halfway across the bar.

"Every fourth or fifth wave is bigger," Maribel explained. "Everyone, grab the rope and get ready to pull." After a short wait, she hollered, "Here they come!"

A pair of waves sailed toward them. They caught the boat and surfed it across the bar into deeper water.

"Climb aboard," Maribel ordered. "We'll use the oars until we get into the mangroves. There's a creek that leads to a small bay—I remember seeing it on the chart. The man won't be able to find us there."

Luke rowed with all his strength toward an opening in the trees. The airboat was a vague dark shape, difficult to see through the rain and dusky light.

The man doesn't have to find us, the boy thought. *His dog will.*

TWENTY-ONE
TRAPPED!

Maribel was right. The opening led to a ribbon of deep water between the trees. The boat's oarlocks creaked with every stroke. Like a water spider, the boat glided the trio around a bend into a bay so shallow that a dozen tall white birds hunted in privacy.

Mangroves stilled the wind. Lightning popped; the sky flickered. Rain poured down in waves, sometimes lightly, sometimes in a soaking deluge.

Every minute or two Sabina would look back and say, "I don't see him. He gave up, don't you think?" More than once, she declared, "I bet that drunkard finally learned his lesson."

Luke wanted to believe her but didn't. The airboat,

with its electric motor, could follow in silence. For all they knew, the bearded man was closing in from the other side of the bushes.

Maribel realized this as well. "We have to stay quiet," she said. "No talking unless we have to. If he can't hear us, he won't know where to look."

The older sister found the chart beneath the console. She studied it and whispered directions while the boy continued to row.

There was another thin cut through the trees. It opened into a bay that, in Luke's mind, resembled a pond. It was rimmed by mangroves, and a cluster of palm trees marked the spiral of a low hill in what seemed to be a swamp.

Maribel had more to worry about than just the shark poacher. She also feared they might have to spend the night in the boat. The sun had dropped below the trees. Overhead, purple-gray clouds absorbed the last of the day's light and warmth. The summer rain suddenly felt as cold as snow.

It was better, she decided, to stop at a place where they could get out, flee from the man, and find a place to hide if necessary. It had to be a spot with high ground. Anywhere else, they would have to slog through muck.

We'll tie up there. Maribel signaled this order by pointing to the hill and mouthing the words.

Using one oar, Luke turned toward the palm trees. The boat nosed into the mangroves. Sabina lashed the front cleat to a low-hanging branch. Maribel dropped the spare anchor off the stern, then touched a finger to her lips. "Don't talk for at least ten minutes," she warned. "If he's coming, we'll hear him. If he gave up, we'll untangle our propeller and start the engine. Okay?"

Sabina's was so cold that her lips were blue. Maribel and Luke were shivering, too. In a forward hatch was the last dry towel. The sisters used it to curl up on the deck, out of the wind, to wait.

Luke? With a wave, Maribel invited the boy to join them and share the towel.

Luke winced at the idea of cuddling close to the Estéban sisters. So he responded in a whisper, "Somebody should stand guard. Don't you think?"

It seemed a good excuse until a haze of mosquitoes descended. Bug spray didn't work in a drizzling rain. The insects bombarded his ears and burned like pepper when their needle-beaks pierced his shirt and every inch of his bare skin. Finally he gave up. Mosquitoes couldn't bite through a towel, so he accepted Maribel's offer. It felt weird at first to squeeze in between two freezing girls. But he was cold, too. The warmth of their bodies felt good through his sodden clothes.

Soon Maribel looped an arm over the boy's chest. This was startling. When Sabina did the same, he decided it was okay. Huddling together on a stormy night was the only way to stay warm. He began to relax. A fresh wave of rain rocked the boat. Mangrove leaves clattered in the wind. After a few drowsy minutes, he might have drifted into sleep but for one thing—he heard the distant barking of a dog.

Next came the muffled voice of a man who ordered the pit bull, "Find those brats!"

Luke sat up. The voice seemed to come from the other side of the island they were on. Not far away.

"What's wrong?" Sabina yawned. "Don't tell me you need that stupid bucket again."

She hadn't heard what the boy had heard.

"Maribel, listen to me," Luke said, giving the girl a shake. "He's on the other side of the island. I know it—and he's coming this way."

"Who, the shark poacher?" The older sister raised her

head, then lay back. "Maybe you were dreaming. No one can hear anything in a storm like this."

In a hurry the boy got to his feet. "It wasn't a dream. Start cutting that rope off the propeller. The dog's after us. If she finds me first, we might be okay. So I'm going to go check."

"Check where?"

"The island," he said.

Maribel sat up. "No! We're staying together, like we're supposed to." She spoke in a harsh whisper.

Luke knelt and spoke into her ear. "I have to. If I don't, the dog will lead the guy straight to us. Then what do we do? The dog likes me—she *wants* to like me, anyway. I'm sure of it. If I can make her trust me, she'll stop barking, and then the guy won't be able to follow her."

The boy sensed the older sister wavering. "I won't be gone long," he promised. "While you're waiting, try the radio again. It can't hurt."

He, too, had been thinking about the airboat's strange antenna. It might have caused the static that prevented their calls for help. Now that the airboat's engine was disabled, maybe their little radio would work.

"I don't like splitting up," Maribel said. "At least take

something to protect yourself with." She reached for the closest weapon she could find—the amber-colored tagging pole—and forced the boy to take it. "It's better than nothing," she said. "And the moment you find that dog—or if it tries to bite you—come straight back here. Understand? I shouldn't let you go at all."

Sabina had been too cold to focus on Luke or what he had planned. She did now. She watched him scamper into the mangroves toward higher ground, carrying the pole as if it were a spear. Her imagination trailed the boy up a steep shell mound to a clearing beneath unseen palm trees.

The girl's hand moved to her necklace. A sense of dread had turned the string of beads to ice.

"The farm boy's right," she whispered to her sister. "We've got to get our engine started. The drunkard's coming—and I think he plans to kill us."

TWENTY-TWO
LIGHTNING STRIKES TWICE

A clearing beneath palm trees, high atop a mound of shells, was unexpected in a mangrove swamp—an Indian mound, just like the mounds where Luke lived. He was pleased after fighting his way uphill through rubbery roots, then briars. There was a breeze up here, and he could see an expanse of water below.

But a hill is a dangerous place to be during a thunderstorm.

"Stay away from trees, and get indoors as fast as you can," he'd been told by every doctor who had examined him.

The same doctors had warned that his grandpa Futch was wrong when he'd claimed, "The same person never gets struck twice."

It *could* happen.

The boy distanced himself from the tallest trees. Using the tagging pole as a cane, he found the mound's highest peak and looked down. Every few seconds a silent flare of lightning brightened his view of the bay. The rumbling darkness that followed gave him time to wonder why the pit bull had stopped barking.

It also gave him time to witness the shark-poaching gang at work.

The fishing trawler he'd seen earlier was anchored in the distance. What he hadn't noticed was a pole attached to the back of the trawler—another strange-looking antenna. It towered above the water. As he watched, something odd happened: A thread of yellow light leaped from the clouds. At the same instant a silver thread shot upward from the antenna. The threads joined into a dazzling burst of lightning that exploded into forks of simmering blue.

Like the flash of a camera, the patterns they created lingered behind Luke's eyes.

He rubbed his eyes, confused. Why hadn't the fishing trawler caught on fire? The vessel had just taken a direct hit yet appeared to be unharmed.

The boy scratched at the burn scar on his shoulder and

thought back to a stormy night in Ohio. He had witnessed something similar there.

Their 4-H meeting had been held in a barn north of Pioneer, the nearest village. When lightning struck the roof of the barn, nothing bad had happened—aside from the noise and a strange metallic odor that had filled the hayloft.

"I bet those lightning rods saved us," their 4-H leader had said while the storm raged above. "Farmers who don't mount lightning rods on their houses and barns are darn fools."

When it was safe, their 4-H leader had led them outside to view three tall steel rods spaced along the highest part of the barn's roof. Each rod was strapped to a copper wire. The wires led to copper stakes buried next to the barn.

Instead of setting the barn on fire, the lightning bolt had zapped one of the rods. The jolt of electricity had followed a wire harmlessly into the ground.

Yes . . . that explained it.

In Luke's mind, the second mystery was solved. The shark poachers had equipped their boats with similar protective rods. That's why they could fish during storms when no one else was out.

Could the strange antennas also interfere with the use of a small radio?

The boy thought about it until he saw something else from the top of the hill. A third boat had arrived. It circled away from the fishing trawler in a slow, methodical way. In his head, he pictured several men dumping a long net off the back of the boat. The net would be strong enough to trap a school of sharks below.

Or was he wrong about a third boat? Maybe it was the airboat. It was possible the bearded man had gotten the engine started and had joined the fishing trawler in deep water.

Luke felt hopeful—until he heard something fast and heavy charging up the mound toward him through brush. He hefted the tagging pole as if it were a spear and backed away. Whatever it was, the thing kept coming. Shells tumbled. A thick branch broke like a rifle shot. He thought about running, but to where? No way would he endanger the sisters by leading the bearded man and his dog back to the rental boat. The man had threatened to beat their butts raw.

Luke stood and faced whatever was charging toward him.

Clouds had muted the last bronze rays of sunset. The light that remained was milky silver, like fog. Beyond the palm trees, bushes churned as something—or someone—tunneled closer. The sound of heavy panting pierced the patter of falling rain.

The boy took a serious gamble. He patted his leg and called, "Here, girl . . . over here. It's me." He spoke in a cooing voice, hoping it was the dog.

The bushes ceased moving. The sound of heavy breathing became a low growl. Then the pit bull launched itself into the clearing on four stiff legs. The animal hesitated. It sniffed the air. The animal's black eyes found Luke, and then it charged, barking wildly.

From shadows below the mound, a man's voice commanded, "Find them brats. Get 'em. I'm on my way!"

Luke started to run but gave up after several long strides. He couldn't outrun a dog. So he turned and waited. When the dog reappeared from the shadows, he took another risk. He crouched low. He placed the tagging pole on the ground, then dropped to his knees so he and the pit bull were at eye level.

The dog noticed. It stopped beneath a palm tree not far away. Its stubby tail wagged briefly. The animal whimpered as if eager to make friends. But it was undecided—probably for fear of the punishment that would come later.

"Good dog . . . good girl," the boy whispered. "Yes, you are." He clapped his hands and spoke sweetly. "Come here, you big baby. Don't listen to your owner. He's nothing but a big bucket load."

The pit bull glanced back, as if it understood. The animal whimpered and whined—then stiffened at the sound of its owner's voice. The dog had no choice but to obey when the man yelled from somewhere nearby, "Don't let 'em go. Sic 'em, you dummy. Why'd you stop barking?"

Fangs bared, the dog crept toward the boy as if stalking wounded prey.

Luke backed away several yards. He knew he should be frightened. But he wasn't—not of the dog. And the bearded man? Luke could probably outrun him. Once again, the boy knelt and spoke softly. He held out his hands to prove he was harmless. Despite this, the pit bull came toward him at a trot, still growling. Its black eyes glittered in the misty light.

Uh-oh. The dog was going to attack no matter what, the boy realized, because that's what it had been commanded to do. Worse, he had abandoned his only weapon.

The tagging pole, with its steel dart, lay on the ground between them, the dog barking wildly now, close enough to leap after a couple of strides and sink its fangs into Luke's throat.

The boy threw his hands up to protect his face. He was spinning away when all the air seemed to be sucked from the sky. Then a blinding flash shattered the tree canopy above. After a sizzling *boom*, a ball of fire and palm fronds rained down as if a bomb had gone off.

"Lightning never strikes the same person twice," Grandpa Futch had promised.

You're wrong, the boy thought in the confusing seconds that followed. He'd been knocked to the ground. A smoky stench burned his eyes—but this time it was different. His skin wasn't on fire. And he could breathe without having to fight for air.

On shaky legs, Luke got up. He double-checked his body parts to confirm he was okay. From the shadows came the crashing sounds of someone running away. He was confused until he figured it out—the bearded man, frightened after nearly being hit by lightning, was retreating downhill.

The boy was sure of it when the shark poacher called

from somewhere near the water, "Come here, dummy. Get back in the boat. Come on, load up—I ain't getting killed on your account."

A brief warbling whistle was the man's final attempt to call a dog that had obeyed his every command. Heavy, splashing footsteps, then the long silence of an electric motor confirmed it. The bearded man, in his broken airboat, was leaving.

Luke stared straight ahead.

Beneath a litter of palm fronds, the pit bull lay on its side, motionless in the clearing.

The boy rushed to the dog. He scooped the weight and warmth of its body into his arms. The animal remained a limp, dense weight. Smoke curled from a burn mark on the dog's neck. Lightning had seared away a patch of hair and left an elaborate forked scar.

The scar resembled what Luke saw every morning in the mirror before he put on a shirt—or hid beneath a pair of gloves.

At his feet lay the tagging pole he'd made from a lightning-shattered tree. The dog had fallen on the thing. The pole's glossy amber wood smoldered. Its steel point flickered with remnants of an intense electrical blast.

Luke focused on the dog. "Hey, girl . . . hey, wake up," he urged. He shook the pit bull and pulled her close so that his cheek was against the dog's muscular head. "You'll be okay . . . Come on—you can't be dead!"

That was a silly thing to say to an animal that wasn't breathing.

"Hey," the boy pleaded, "don't leave me." He loosened the dog's heavy steel-studded collar. "Open your eyes and take a breath."

That, too, was a childish hope. Animals zapped by lightning do not awaken to take a last breath.

The pit bull suddenly seemed light, not heavy, when Luke walked away cradling the dog in his arms. It was as surprising as the stillness that accompanied the two of them down the mound, through the mangroves.

"Thank god!" Maribel said when she saw the boy. "Hurry up. I finally talked to Hannah on the radio. She's on her way. Where's the man with the beard? Is he still chasing us?"

The girl sounded frantic but calmed when Luke responded with a slow shake of his head.

The sisters had already cut the anchor rope free from the propeller. The rental boat's motor fired immediately when Maribel turned the key.

"What happened to this poor thing?" Sabina demanded. Luke had handed her the dog's body before climbing aboard.

"Lightning," he said.

"Lightning—that's all?" The girl reacted as if it were no big deal. "Let me hold him on the way back."

"She's a female pit bull, not a male," Luke corrected the girl.

"Okay, then I'll hold *her*. Is she dead?"

"She's not breathing. What do you think?" The boy felt numb as he looked down at the dog lying in Sabina's lap.

He had been crying—crying for the first time since his mother's funeral. But that was okay. In the dim late-afternoon light, rain would keep it a secret between just him and his two trusted friends.

"That shark poacher's nothing but a coward," the boy said. They had cleared the mangroves at idle speed. He was standing shoulder to shoulder with Maribel. "The jerk ran away, went off and left his dog—didn't care if she was buried or not." He glanced toward the smoky distance where the airboat was making slow progress toward the fishing trawler. "We've got nothing to worry about now."

The shark poacher does, Maribel thought. But she said, "Let him run. He won't get far. You were right about the radio. It works fine now. Why don't you call Hannah again and tell her what happened? It'll save her a trip. Yes, please call her. She can wait at the marina for the police."

"As if that stupid detective will believe anything we say," Sabina grumbled. Her necklace of blue and yellow beads were now around the dog's neck. The girl sniffed, leaned closer, and whispered something into the stillness of the pit bull's pointed ear.

Maribel managed a wise half smile. She touched a pocket of her shorts to make sure the waterproof camera was safe, then placed her hand on the throttle.

"The police will believe us this time," she said. Then she ordered her crew to "*Hold on!*"

The young captain steered their boat toward home.

TWENTY-THREE
THE PRICE OF FAME, AND A STOLEN DOG

Sabina was in a foul mood despite all the good things that had happened in the week since they had survived the storm and the shark poacher's attack.

At the request of a reporter, she had written a new poem. That's why she was upset. She'd been struggling to translate the poem into English before a Tampa Bay television crew arrived. Now she was running out of time.

How can they expect me to write beautifully in only twenty minutes? the girl fumed.

In truth, the reporters didn't care if she wrote beautifully. They only pretended to enjoy poems by the "fearless child poet" who had helped bust the largest ring of shark poachers in Florida.

Sabina had done enough interviews in the last few days to know the truth. All they really wanted her to do was smile, look into a camera, and answer their confusing questions in only a sentence or two—and please stop asking reporters if a makeup kit could be provided.

Reporters were always in a hurry. They were always on something called a deadline. It was such a mean-sounding word that the girl had gone to the trouble of finding it in an English dictionary. The first definition she found was boring: *the latest time by which a project must be completed.* The second definition, however, revealed the true meanness of the word. *Deadline: a line around a prison beyond which prisoners are liable to be shot.*

Shot?

No wonder reporters didn't care about beautiful things such as proper makeup or the music of words on paper.

Sabina's temper had gotten the best of her on two occasions. What was the use of being famous if she couldn't share the story of their shark team in verse? But when she'd read a poem in Spanish to a reporter from Orlando and a blog columnist from New York, they had only smiled in puzzlement and nodded politely.

Why? Because they hadn't understood a single line!

Sabina was alone in her room, sitting with her diary open. On the nightstand, a candle from the shop in Havana flickered. It was a bright, warm day in June, yet the candle was necessary, as the women in white had taught her. Candlelight helped set the proper mood for writing poetry. But the time, according to her almost-new iPhone, was nearly four o'clock. She had only fifteen minutes until the crew from Tampa arrived!

Impossible, the girl thought. *The world would be a happier place if everyone spoke Spanish and people weren't afraid of being shot because of deadlines.*

The girl was tempted to give up. She'd spent an hour trying to find the perfect last word for the final line of her poem, and she had failed. It had to rhyme with the English word *complicated*. She had found several words that fit—*skated, dated, overrated*—yet none carried the deeper meaning of what she wanted to say.

No wonder poets often die lonely and alone, she thought. In her case, penniless and in jail, too—if, a week ago, that stubborn detective hadn't agreed to view Maribel's video of the shark poacher's airboat attack.

Scowling, the girl fidgeted and chewed at the eraser on her pencil. She doodled a picture that resembled a shark fin. She checked her iPhone for the thousandth time, hoping to receive her first text message.

Disappointment—*again*.

She was reaching for the dictionary when her room rocked with the wake of a slow passing boat. This was a good excuse to get up and part the curtains. Outside, in the harbor, Captain Hannah was at the wheel of her fancy little charter boat. Seated in front, next to the curly-haired retriever, was Luke. He wore fishing shorts and a handsome blue T-shirt with gold lettering—but no gloves.

Typical, Sabina thought. *The TV reporters will be so impressed by his lightning tattoos, they won't have time to hear a stupid poem I can't finish anyway.*

Instantly the girl scolded herself for being unfair. Luke didn't care about publicity. He hated the attention they had received since, four days earlier, the bearded man and members of his gang were seen in handcuffs on national TV.

And there was another more important reason. It had

to do with a promise that Luke, Maribel, and Sabina had made that night, after the storm—and a secret they now all shared.

Remembering that secret caused the girl to think back. Slowly her frown was replaced by the smile of a writer who had stumbled onto a good idea.

Luke unknowingly might have provided the last two words in the poem she'd been laboring to finish.

Or had he?

The girl hunched over her diary. She scribbled and erased, scribbled and erased some more, until she was finally satisfied. Then, in a whisper, she reread what she'd written, to see if her words touched a poetic chord.

An Ode to Truth

Instead of thanking the farm boy
For solving the bearded man's plot
The detective proved he doesn't know squat
A nice man, true, who thought me a liar
Even after lightning nearly set us on fire
If the detective had spent more days afloat
He might have known, "The poachers use
   airboats!"

Instead, for him, the problem was too complicated
*Until the mystery was solved by . . . **Sharks***
Incorporated

Yes. It was the perfect ending to a poem that was broodingly musical in Spanish. But it was also pretty good in the language Americans call English.

Sabina closed her diary. She ignored the stupid mirror in the hall and hurried out to greet a large white van from Tampa Bay 10 News.

Maribel had already decided to let her sister do most of the talking to the news crew. Good captains, after all, put the happiness of their crew before their own. She didn't mind. It would be fun answering questions from stylish folding chairs on a portable stage where a camera with wheels zoomed in and out.

Before the interview started, the reporter—a woman named Jay-Cee—encouraged onlookers to come closer and form an audience. Dozens of people soon made a semicircle around the stage. The number increased when the Everglades Sea Camp bus parked and discharged a bunch of teenage passengers.

On the stage to Maribel's left was a TV monitor. The screen showed what viewers would see: Sabina and herself with Dinkins Bay in the background.

When some of the campers began chanting "We want Luke . . . we want Luke," the camera zoomed in to show the only empty chair on stage.

"Think we should wait a little longer?" Jay-Cee asked the girls. She was pleased by the audience's reaction. "Sounds to me like your missing teammate has a lot fans. I bet they'd love to hear what he has to say. Should we wait?"

Sabina glanced toward the shed, where, she suspected, the farm boy was hiding. "Not if you're on deadline, that's for sure," the girl responded. "Or unless you brought lights—it'll be dark in an hour or two." Her voice boomed through the microphone that was pinned to her blouse.

Maribel waited for the laughter to die down. She, too, wore a mic, so she spoke softly. "Luke has to meet with a police detective this afternoon," she explained. "He asked me to apologize. It was sort of a last-minute thing."

This would have been more accurate if Maribel had

admitted something else: It would have taken a tractor to drag the boy onto the stage now that the Sea Campers had arrived.

"Meeting with police. That's interesting," the reporter said. She made a rolling motion with her hand to signal the camera operators. Red lights atop the cameras blinked on before she asked Maribel, "Would you mind repeating what you just said about Luke? We're taping now."

Maribel did.

"Hmm . . . Luke's not here because he's meeting privately with a police detective." Jay-Cee smiled. "That's *very* interesting. Do you think it might have something to do with the fifty-thousand-dollar reward offered by Ocean Environmental? Wouldn't that be great? After all, who deserves it more than the kids who busted the biggest shark-poaching ring in the state?"

The audience applauded while the Sea Campers stomped and whistled.

Jay-Cee was energized by their enthusiasm. "What do you think, Maribel? I was told that it's up to the police to decide who gets the reward. Maybe Luke will have some good news for you"—she motioned to the covey of Sea Campers in the front row—"and his many fans."

"Maybe," Maribel said.

"I sure hope so," Sabina chimed in agreeably.

But the truth about Luke's meeting with Detective Miller, as both sisters knew, had to remain a secret.

The boy had been accused of lying about a missing pit bull that had been struck and killed by lightning.

Now the bearded man was demanding that the police either find the dog or charge Luke with theft. Maybe even arrest him.

When the Everglades Sea Camp bus was gone and the TV cameras were done, Luke slapped his thigh and shared a silent command with Pete, the curly-haired retriever: *Heel*.

The dog trotted at his side until the boy pointed and urged, *Swim*.

Pete galloped toward the dock, scattering gulls and terns. He vaulted high into the air, crashed down with a splash, and resurfaced, spouting water from his nose.

The boy was surprised to find Maribel waiting for him on the steps to the laboratory.

"You're just in time," she said. "Detective Miller went to

get something out of his car. My mother gave him permission to speak to us, and Hannah did, too. Luke . . . where have you been?"

"Cripes, you mean he's still here? He's mad about me being late, I suppose." Luke, who was seldom late, had intentionally tried to avoid this meeting, and the Tampa 10 TV News. "How'd it go?"

"The interview? Fine," Maribel said. "Don't worry about that now. He isn't mad, just concerned. The shark poacher hates us. That's probably why he's causing all this trouble about the dog. But the police can't take sides. They have a job to do. Luke"—the girl looked into his eyes—"the detective said he needs more proof that what we said is true. I think he came here because he wants to help."

"Came to arrest me, more likely," Luke scowled. His attention moved from the dock to the lab. The biologist and his seaplane had yet to return. "Where's Sabina?"

"Still with the TV crew from Tampa," Maribel said. "She wrote a new poem. The reporter didn't want to hear it, but the poor woman finally gave in. You know how pushy my sister can be. Anyway . . . I thought it was best if I come here alone. I was surprised to find the detective still waiting for you."

Luke looked toward the path to the parking lot. "Probably went to his car to get handcuffs, you think?

"No," the girl said gently. "He said he has something he wants us to see. Me too, I guess. But he wanted you to be here."

Maribel hesitated, then did something that, for her, was bold. She stood and, before the boy could pull away, gave him a reassuring hug. "We're all in this together," she said. "Sabina and I talked about it. We aren't going to let you take the blame for something we all did. Besides, I was in charge of the boat that night."

"Blame for what? We told the truth." Luke said this in a flat tone without emotion. But the way he looked into Maribel's dark, bright eyes communicated a secret they shared. "The pit bull got struck by lightning. She stopped breathing, and we did our best to save her. And that jerk didn't even come back to bury her." The boy turned away, adding, "I suppose now he wants to dig up her grave, huh? The police believed us—until today. I wonder what happened?"

The girl started to respond, then whispered, "Quiet. Here he comes."

The bulky silhouette of the detective came down the path toward them.

TWENTY-FOUR
FORTUNE AND A
SPIKED COLLAR

When the detective returned from his car, he handed Maribel and Luke the front page from the island newspaper.

"This won't be out until tomorrow," the detective said, "so I had the editor slip me a couple of copies. I thought you might like to have them framed. What do you think? I picked them up on the way here."

Luke, who had been expecting handcuffs, looked over Maribel's shoulder. Together, they read the headline at the top of the page:

Police Credit Kids for Busting International Fin Ring
Detective Apologizes, says $50,000 Reward on Its Way

Maribel felt a little dizzy. She knew the reward was a possibility but hadn't allowed herself to think about it.

Luke looked up at the detective "You apologized? Why? We're not mad at you."

"You should be," the detective said. "Especially Maribel and her little sister. I was so sure you kids were . . . well, exaggerating. I felt like an idiot when I finally saw the video you shot. That took a heck of a lot of courage, young lady. Quick thinking, too."

Video of the bearded man in his airboat had confirmed that he had not only threatened the children but had nearly rammed their rental boat. On camera, he had also said more than enough to prove he'd been poaching shark fins.

Maribel was embarrassed by the detective's kind words. "Using the camera was the only way I could make you believe us."

"Which is my fault—that guy could've killed you all," Detective Miller said. He turned to Luke. "I owe you an apology, too. Maybe you forgot, but a couple of our officers laughed when you told us that the poachers used airboats and only fished during lightning storms."

No, Luke hadn't forgotten. The conversation had taken

place a week ago, after the shark poacher's attack. The kids had returned to the marina, wet, cold, eaten up by mosquitoes, but eager to share their story with the police.

The police weren't so easily convinced. Neither the detective nor anyone else had believed their story—particularly Luke's theory about netting sharks during storms. The boy hadn't been confident enough to argue. They were adults, trained police officers. So, yeah, he'd figured it was just another one of his dumb ideas—until Grandpa Futch heard about what Luke had seen.

"Boy, you might be smarter than you look," the old man had said. That was two days after their return. Maribel and Sabina had paid their first visit to the house where Luke and his grandfather lived. The four of them were sitting, drinking sweet iced tea on the porch.

"Modern police don't know a dang thing about old-timey ways of breakin' laws," the man had told them. "There was many a barrel of illegal whiskey smuggled into this state during rainstorms. And that ain't all that was smuggled." Luke's grandfather loved to talk, so he had gone into detail, saying, "That's right, smugglers all up and down this coast. Used to be I didn't get in my boat unless I heard a big boom of thunder. Cops don't get paid enough to risk a lightning storm. Now you go back there and tell that detective your grandpa says he's full of beans."

"Beans?" Sabina had asked, confused.

Maribel had understood, and she posed a delicate question. "You used to be a smuggler, Captain Futch? What did you smuggle?"

The old man hadn't expected this from a pretty, polite girl with a Spanish accent. He had cleared his throat and reached for his empty coffee mug. "Course, I weren't no smuggler. Why, smuggling stuff, that's against the law, young lady. But I *knew* some fellas that did. Bunch of 'em. All I meant was, my grandson here is smarter than folks give him credit for."

Getting up to pour more coffee, the old man had continued to evade by asking, "Luke, did you ever tell these girls what to do if they're on a boat that sinks with livestock aboard?"

For half an hour the old man had held court, talking about the intelligence of pigs compared to horses. Next, he had discussed the virtues of cats, saying he would never again allow a flea-bitten dog into his house. But pigs and cats, by golly, they were welcome.

Now, a week later, Detective Miller confirmed that Luke had been right all along about the shark poachers.

"Instead of laughing at you," the detective said, "we should have listened. We were fools not to. So guess who's not laughing now?"

He turned from Luke to Maribel, who was sitting on the steps to the lab. "This boy figured out what trained investigators from a dozen different departments failed to realize. You both deserve an apology—and my thanks. How about it, Luke?"

The man reached and shook the boy's hand, standing almost eye to eye. Maribel grinned—and wished she'd brought a camera.

For Luke, it felt pretty good shaking the hand of an actual police detective. The boy appreciated the compliment, yet feared it was intended to soften more questions about the missing pit bull.

"Lucky guess," he muttered. "It's not often I figure out much of anything."

The detective studied the boy, puzzled—or suspicious. "A kid as smart as you?" he said finally. "I'm not sure I believe that. But keep this in mind, son . . . I *want* to believe everything you tell me from here on out."

As expected, the man was referring to the shark poacher's complaint about the missing dog.

"I hope you do believe me," the boy replied.

The detective thought this was an odd response. After another long look of concern, he let it go. "When I really felt like a fool was when we arrested the woman in the black van and the old guy in the wheelchair. Turns out they're all part of the gang. Criminals tend to be convincing liars, which good cops are supposed to know. But I fell for their sob story anyway."

The man reached for his briefcase, still talking. "What it comes down to," he said, "is that you kids were right from the very start. So I spoke to the editor of the island paper this morning and did what I should've done last week—apologized to you publicly. You three earned that reward. Luke"—the briefcase snapped open—"I wish that was the end of the story. But it's not. You already know the reason why."

The boy nodded. "The guy claims I stole his dog."

"It's more than just talk now. The guy had his attorney file a complaint against you yesterday. Listen to me closely—the attorney provided us with what the owner claims is proof that his dog's still alive. I want to believe you kids, I really do. But you're going to have to explain how a dog that was supposedly killed by lightning is still running around loose on Sanibel."

"*What?*"

"You heard me, son."

Luke was a terrible liar. He knew it, so he stared at the ground while Maribel said, "That's a strange thing for them to claim. What kind of proof?"

The detective held up a tiny electronic device. "This kind of proof. This is a GPS tracker. The owner claims the pit bull was specially trained—worth a couple thousand dollars. So he had a chip—a tiny transmitter—inserted into the dog's collar."

"His *collar*?" For the first time Maribel sounded worried.

"Afraid so," the man said. "There's a satellite service that pet owners use. I looked it up. For a few bucks a month, owners can track their pet up to three thousand miles away. Ever hear of such a thing?"

Yes, Luke had. The Angus cattle he'd raised in 4-H had carried a similar chip behind the left ear. "If the bearded guy cared so much about his dog," the boy countered, "why'd he go off and leave her on an island during a storm?"

"He abused that poor animal," Maribel insisted. "On the video I took, you heard him—he called the dog 'dummy.' And some other names too nasty to repeat. Then he ordered the dog to attack us and went off and left the poor thing to be struck by lightning. And the dog *was* struck by lightning. I swear."

"That's not easy to believe, but I guess I do," the detective said. "Personally, I think the owner just wants revenge. You kids outsmarted him—a thief who's been arrested too many times to count. He'd come up with what he thought was a brilliant scheme to get rich smuggling shark fins. And he would've gotten rich if you kids hadn't made him look like a fool. Thing is, Luke"—the detective tapped a button on the GPS tracking device in his hand—"the law is the law. I'll help you kids as much as I can. But first you're going to have to explain this."

He turned the little electronic screen for Luke and Maribel to see. It showed a satellite map of Sanibel Island. A patch of blue water was Dinkins Bay. A tiny red light pulsed near the shoreline. The pulsing light wasn't far from where they sat on the steps of the lab.

"That blinking light indicates the location of the pit bull's collar," the detective said. "If the dog were dead, he wouldn't be swimming around out there in the bay, now would he?"

The man expected a response. Instead, Luke stared at the ground.

The detective was getting impatient. "Look, kids. My advice is to tell the truth and cooperate. I promise you that the pit bull will be safe until a judge decides what's best. So, Luke"—the detective lowered the tracking device—"do us all a favor and call the dog. Okay?"

Luke looked at Maribel. The girl sighed and said softly, "If Luke's a thief, then I'm a thief, too. We didn't know the pit bull wore a special collar."

"Obviously not," the detective replied. "I know you did what you did for the best of reasons—but it was illegal." The man seemed sympathetic but again had to insist, "Call the dog, Luke. I'll stick around until animal control comes to take him to the pound. I'm sorry, but that's the way it has to be."

Luke did as he'd been told. He whistled, then whistled again. Soon a dog appeared from the mangroves, sopping wet, and charged toward them. The animal showered the detective with saltwater, then sat panting at the boy's side.

But the dog was a curly-haired retriever, not a pit bull.

"Wait . . . what's going on here?" Detective Miller demanded. "That's the wrong dog." He consulted the tracking device and became more confused. "But it *has* to be the same dog, according to this. I wouldn't call it a pit bull, but he belongs to the shark poacher, right?"

"Nope," Luke said. He was struggling to unbuckle something from the retriever's neck. "This dog belongs to Dr. Ford. If the bearded guy wants me arrested for stealing something, I guess you can arrest me for stealing *this*."

The boy held up a thick leather collar that was dotted with metal spikes.

"That's all?"

Luke, then Maribel, responded with a shrug.

The detective released a long, slow breath, a big smile on his face. "Let me see that thing."

Luke handed him the leather collar. "After the pit bull was struck by lightning, I took this off, hoping she'd start breathing again. Maribel's sister even tried some kind of magic spell—like, she's a witch, you know? Silly kid stuff. That dog *was* hit by lightning, Detective Miller. I shouldn't have put the collar on another dog, I guess. If I give it back, are you still going to arrest me?"

"Took the collar, why?" the man wanted to know. "As a souvenir?"

Luke said, "Sorta," which was somewhat true.

The detective began to laugh, then laughed harder when he searched the collar and found the transmitter. It was sewn into a pocket of leather. "This is one of the funniest mix-ups ever. I'm surprised you kids didn't notice the little chip here."

Maribel didn't trust herself to look at Luke, who, days ago, *had* noticed the transmitter chip. On the same day, the boy had declared that helping an abused animal could not be considered stealing.

The detective was suddenly in a good mood. He used his phone to snap several pictures of the pit bull's collar, then put the phone away. "I can't wait to pay that shark poacher a visit, and prove how wrong he was. Maybe the guy will learn his lesson finally and never cross you kids again."

Maribel didn't speak until the detective was gone. "Luke," she said, "do you think anyone will ever find out the truth?"

The boy consulted the wisdom of his lightning eye to confirm the detective's car was pulling away. "I don't know," he responded, then grinned in a confidential way. "It depends on how mad my grandpa gets if he catches that pit bull sleeping in my bed."